THE DOG

Scott Baker Sweeney

authorHOUSE®

AuthorHouse™
1663 Liberty Drive
Bloomington, IN 47403
www.authorhouse.com
Phone: 833-262-8899

Published by AuthorHouse 10/29/2020

ISBN: 978-1-6655-0555-0 (sc)
ISBN: 978-1-6655-0553-6 (hc)
ISBN: 978-1-6655-0554-3 (e)

Library of Congress Control Number: 2020921089

Print information available on the last page.

The shortest distance between two points is a straight line. That may be true, but it's not always achievable to the common traveler, especially if the mode of transportation is an automobile. Two examples are the cities of Evanston, Illinois and Bloomington, Indiana, where no straight-line highway exists. Selecting a route utilizing multiple state highways was a familiar and minor inconvenience for Dr. Cadwallader Wells. He made this trek hundreds of times from Evanston while attending Indiana University as well as several times post-graduation.

However, on this particular trip in the summer of 2016 it would dramatically impact and change his life!

Every year for the last eleven, Dr. Wells, or Caddy

as friends would call him would make this drive from Evanston to Bloomington to attend his annual fraternity brothers golf outing. The outing was always on the third Sunday in July and at a prestigious private golf club on the outskirts of Bloomington. Caddy would generally drive down on the Saturday before and stay overnight at a hotel. This year was no different.

The last few rays from the setting sun warmed the right side of the Doctor's face as he was somewhere south of Lafayette.

"Oh no!" He muttered to himself, as up ahead he spotted large orange triangle signs adorning the side of the road.

"This is never good! Road signs never have anything good to report." Within moments his initial reaction would become reality.

'Road Closed Ahead' 'Bridge Out' 'Detour'

For the first time ever, Dr. Cadwallader Wells will rely on his IPhone navigation app. to get him to his destination. So, he exits his familiar highway and heads East on a road which he has never driven.

The sun was now down, and the detour signs were flashing, but despite their illumination he somehow missed his initial turn. He was now totally dependent on his device but enjoying the new scenery just the same.

"This truly is Americana", he thought as he passed through yet another small town. But the warm feeling he experienced was soon replaced with loneliness brought on by miles of rural pavement and reduced visibility. Caddy had not switched his headlights from high beam for miles, as he had not encountered an oncoming vehicle for some time.

"Shouldn't I be getting a verbal command from my phone to turn south by now?" He was starting to have concerns that his direction App on his phone was not operating correctly.

Another town in the distance, as indicated by the amber glow on the dark horizon. *'North Salem Ahead'* was the sign he just passed.

"There has to be a crossroad in that town", he thought as he looked down to study his phone. "Yes!" He declared, confirming his find. Caddy looked down again to study the phone map but dwelled too long. When he looked up he wasn't prepared for what was standing in the middle of the road. Adrenalin took over sending panic flooding to his brain. As a reaction he turned the steering wheel sharp to the left and stomped on the brake. Despite his reduced speed the car veered and left the road, sliding down an embankment then coming to rest against a large tree.

After a momentary sense of relief that the wild ride was over and a brief self-examination, panic resumed.

"Oh my God, did I hit him?" The grim thought quickly consumed him. Caddy urgently removed his safety belt and threw open the door. A few steps from his car he took a deep breath and relaxed, as at the top of the hill stood a large dog, looking back down at him. The dog wagged his tail and barked, as if to greet him to his town. Then he turned and walked away from sight. Dr. Wells stood motionless, looking at his car, and then back up at the road. The dog reappeared and barked again, this time turning his head away and then back at the Dr., as if he wanted him to follow. Caddy sensed the K9's desires and did so.

When he climbed up the embankment and reached the road the dog was not there, instead he was several hundred feet away. Once again, the dog barked and wagged his tail, so Caddy followed. The dog never let him catch up. He remained in sight, but always at a guarded distance. It was apparent to the Doctor that the dog indeed was leading him somewhere. Hopefully, to a 24-hour wrecker service or local law enforcement, he thought to himself. Calling 911 was never a consideration and now it wasn't a valid option either. When he reached in his pockets and there was no phone, he realized that he left it in the car. The car now several blocks away, he wasn't about to turn around to retrieve it.

Sidewalks illumined by streetlamps and a bright crescent moon would now serve as Caddy's path to rectify his precarious situation, or at least he hoped that to be the case. After walking for a couple of blocks in front of old Victorian style homes and large Tulip trees he could now see downtown. In his view now was the business district, a well-lit block of two-story brick buildings, with a few cars paralleling the curb. In reaction to this sight he increased the gate of his walk.

Apparently, the dog wasn't interested in going downtown! He stopped, looked back to confirm Caddy was still in pursuit, and then darted through a gate, down a walk and up onto the porch of this beautiful two story early Grand Victorian home. Seconds later, Caddy arrived at the gate.

Pearl Street Bed and Breakfast was the name engraved on a brass sign at the entrance gate.

Looking down the brick walk and up onto the porch sat the red dog.

"Is this where you live boy?" Caddy spoke out

to the dog and he replied with a *WOOF!* "Do you want me to come up there?" The dog stood up, wagging his tail with delight.

Regardless of the dog's jovial approval, the exterior of the house was certainly inviting for Caddy, with its gas lights and hanging flowerpot arrangements. The lights were on in every room which added warmth to the quaint ambiance.

Doctor Wells proceeded down the walk and up the steps toward a large stained-glass door. When arriving at the porch landing at the top of the steps, he expected to be greeted by his new four-legged friend, but the dog was nowhere in sight. He didn't ponder the dog's sudden vanishing act, but instead reached out and rang the doorbell. While he waited on someone to arrive at the door he stared out over the yard, looking around to see if he could spot the dog.

"Can I help you?" Caddy spun around to find an old woman standing in the doorway. In her left hand she was holding a coffee cup, but in right hand, limp at her side, she was gripping a pistol.

"What are you looking for" She sternly inquired.

Caddy stood there frozen for a few seconds unable to audibly produce an appropriate response. Just as she was raising her right arm, he spoke.

"Good evening madam, I was just looking for your dog, while I waited for the door. He was just here." Caddy was a bit nervous, not expecting a gun wielding individual to greet him, especially at a bed and breakfast.

"I don't have a damn dog!" she scolded. "But I do have a Colt revolver and I'm not afraid to use it! So, if you're one of those Meth-heads that moved to the outskirts of town, I suggest that you move along."

"I am sorry, I didn't mean to frighten you! I'm not from around here. My name is Doctor Cadwallader Wells, I swerved my car to miss this dog and ended up running off the road and into a tree." Caddy stood awkwardly pointing out to the road. The woman relaxed her arm, so that the steel barrel was now pointing toward the floor.

"What the hell kinda name is Cadwallader? She sarcastically blurted out. "And, you don't look like no damn doctor to me!" She stood there studying him.

"I have identification. Caddy reached for his wallet, pulled out his driver's license and hospital identification card. "I don't think that my car is damaged beyond drivability, so I just need a tow truck to pull me back up the hill and to the road. Is there someone in town that I can call?

"That would be Ron Goode." She mumbled, responding to his question but didn't elaborate, or even looked up as she was engrossed studied his identification cards.

"I was heading downtown, but this dog, the same dog that I nearly hit, enticed me to your door instead." As soon as that sentence left his mouth, Caddy wished that he would have left out the part about enticing him to her door and was now preparing for her retort. She looked up, walked closer and looked directly into his eyes, while simultaneously handing him back his cards.

"What color was this dog?" She asked with a deep sober tone.

"It was a red Dog, I think a Labrador Retriever. He was just standing right here on your porch! He has to be around here somewhere, it's not like he could disappear."

"Mercy, my God!" she softly declared. Please come in Doctor." Suddenly the woman's demeaner completely changed. She was visibly shook by Caddy's account of events. She turned around as if to enter her home but stopped and leaned against the doorframe to stabilize herself. Caddy was concerned that she was about to faint.

"Are you okay ma'am? Let's get you inside. The doctor reached under her arms and guided her into the house. "You are a bit wobbly. Let's sit down and let me take a look at you! Also, can we just set that revolver on the table for a bit?" Instead, she handed it to him and he did the task for her. The physician in

Caddy instinctively took over, as he started asking her about heart history and her medicines.

"I'm okay son, everyone in this town has been a bit under the weather with the flue lately. I'm probably just catching that."

Caddy helped her to a couch, sat down beside her and began looking her over.

"I have an emergency medical bag in my trunk, I could go get it, but we really should call 911 and have an ambulance take you to a hospital and have them look you over."

She shook her head. "No, I'm not going to no damn hospital! I feel better already. The truth is, I guess that I got a little light-headed hearing of your encounter with the Red Dog. By-the-way, sorry about making that comment about your name!" Caddy drew back and looked at her funny.

"Red Dog encounter!? I'm confused, but you can explain later. And, don't worry about the name, I've heard that all my life. I'm the fourth generation Cadwallader, you can just call me Caddy, my friends do." Caddy brought the conversation back around to her health.

Let's at lease call the EMT's and have them give you the once over. I would have already called, but my phone is also back in my car.

"I'll tell you what Doc., I'll call and get that wrecker to pull you back on the road, then you can retrieve your bag, look me over and in return I'll give you a room for the night."

"Okay, thank you, but if I find something that concerns me, you are off to the hospital. Caddy continued. Thanks for the room offer, I'll take a raincheck, I need to get to Bloomington. By the way, in the confusion, I didn't catch your name."

Her face turned red with embarrassment. "I am so sorry, how rude of me. She extended her hand. "Myrna Wilson at your service." Myrna leaned over and grabbed the phone sitting on the end table and began to dial.

After a few minutes of banter on the phone she

hung up. "Ron's on the way. You will have to meet him there."

"Is there anyone here in the house who can sit with you, while I go meet him?"

"You doctor are wearing on my nerves. I will be fine, go to your car. He will be there probably before you!"

Caddy stood up and walked over to the door.

"Hey Doctor, it was very nice to meet you! It just occurred to me that you are probably the first doctor to set foot in this house, since the original owner Doc. Wiseheart."

Caddy spun around and replied. "Maybe I will, take you up on that room! You still owe me an explanation about that Red Dog." He hesitated a moment longer. "And, you can also tell me about Doc. Wiseheart."

68 Years Earlier

"Morty, I'm home" The word 'home' was audibly blocked by the bang sound made by the front-screen door slamming as Doc Wiseheart entered his house. No matter of the incomplete sentence, the sound of his voice gave her all the notification she needed.

"I'm in the kitchen Dear!" Responded his bride.

Doctor Oscar Wiseheart and his wife Morty were married right after he graduated from the University of Louisville School of Medicine. They moved in with Morty's parents in North Salem, with the aspirations of starting a family medical practice as well as a family.

North Salem was a thriving farm community and because of this, despite the Great Depression they were able to re-establish their collapsed bank earlier than many metropolitan banks throughout the country.

As with all small towns across America, North Salem needed a physician and right then they were without. The bonus to this scenario was that Oscar Wiseheart's wife was family. She has several relatives who lived there including her parents and siblings. The community was more than accommodating to the young Doctor Wiseheart enticing him to stay. This includes the North Salem State Bank, who allowed him to practice rent free for a year in a small building downtown, which they repossessed just three years earlier. The bank also loaned him money to build their grand home just one year after starting his practice.

Today was a very important day of celebration, not just for North Salem, but for all of America. It was Sunday afternoon, September 9th, 1948, three years after the end of World War II, and the town was having a parade.

The Doctor entered the kitchen to find his wife cloaked in a full-length white apron, which served as a layer of protection to a fashionable blue dress that she wore beneath. She was icing a cake that she had retrieved from the oven an hour earlier.

"Oh good you are home! I was worried that when you left after church to check on Mrs. Hamilton you may get delayed from accompanying me at the parade today. So how is Katherine?" Morty inquired.

"Maybe, not so good!" He paused to collect his thoughts. "She has me puzzled.

I need to run her to the hospital for further evaluation. She has a mass in her lower abdomen, it's larger than an undeveloped fetus, but no appendages, as with a predeveloped baby. She either has a tumor, or she's pregnant with twins. Let's pray for the latter!"

"Oh, Dear God!" Morty immediately stopped what she was doing, dropping her spatula on the countertop. She stood motionless, with her mouth gaping, looking shocked.

North Salem was your typical small town in the 1940's, with a population of around 500 residents. If you lived within the city limits, or a five-mile circumference of, you were either related, close friends, or at the very least mutually acquainted. Katherine Hamilton wasn't just a patient of her husband, Doctor Wiseheart, she was a close friend!

"I couldn't persuade her into going to the hospital today, she wanted to try and celebrate with the rest of the town. Her abdominal pain and nausea comes and goes, hopefully it will subside long enough for her to enjoy today's festivities.

Doc's attention suddenly diverted away from their conversation to the freshly iced cake resting on the counter.

"That's not for you! I'm dropping this off at the church for the reception after the parade. Your cake is next week!" She winked at him. "Someone I know has a birthday next week!" Morty added a melody to her statement and repeated it several times, taunting her husband.

"I'll take the cake, but you can keep the birthday! I've decided to stop having them." He chuckled. "Take off that apron Mrs. Wiseheart and let's go find a good seat to enjoy the parade!"

There's nothing more patriotic than a small-town parade, especially if its commemorating something as momentous as the end of a World War, the end of an evil dictator, and of course peace!

The Wiseheart's did get a front row seat, and right beside the Hamilton's, Bob and Katherine. Doc intentionally sought them out as he wanted to keep an eye on Katherine. It was a good thing that he did, as a third of the way through the ceremony Katherine became light-headed and sick to her stomach. Doc had help from a host of the concerned community who witnessed Katherine's spell, all persuading her into taking a trip to the hospital then and not wait another day. Most significantly Katherine could not refuse the request of both Morty and her husband Robert!

So, Robert rushed home and got his silver Packard and returned via a side street, off the parade route. Doc helped him get Katherine into the car, then the four of them headed for the hospital, a thirty-minute drive. North Salem could barely afford a firetruck and a Police car, so there was no ambulance to call.

The trip was not in vain, Bob and Morty spent the next four hours waiting nervously in the waiting room. When finally, Doc came wheeling Katherine out into the lobby, and they were both smiling from ear to ear they immediately knew that the prognosis was good. They jumped up from their seats and hurried over to greet them.

"Well Mrs. Hamilton shall I tell them, or would you like to do the honor?" Katherine twisted around in her wheelchair.

"Go right ahead Doctor!"

With that command, Doc stopped pushing the chair and came around to the front, so that he and Katherine could make eye contact.

"Very well, the x-rays confirmed that there isn't a large mass below Katherine's stomach, it's actually two small masses. Congratulations Robert, you and Katherine are going to be the parents of twins!"

Katherine sprung from her chair to be caught by her husband. They embraced, tears fell and Morty clapped.

"Easy you two, remember what I said, for the next several weeks you need to take it easy, lots of rest, no heavy lifting and watch what you eat! Right now, in this stage of pregnancy the fetuses are positioned right next to your digestive tract, causing you discomfort." Katherine wiped the tears from her eyes and both she and Bob nodded their heads confirming they understood his orders.

"Morty, let's get the proud new parents to their car so that they can drive us home!" Doc nudged the three toward the exit.

"How about taking us by the church first, God has blessed us, and I want to share the good news with our family and friends!" Katherine looked at Doc for his approval.

"So, the church it is!" Doc's reply was met with cheers

from the small group as they headed back to North Salem.

Six months later, Doctor Wiseheart would deliver the Hamilton's twin girls, and with the help of a new assistant that he would meet for the first time on his birthday.

As promised, Morty did make her husband a birthday cake, and eventually presented it to him along with a very special gift.

It was Sunday and a rainy one at that. Doc and Morty had just got home from church. Once through the door, he sauntered off to his study and she to the kitchen.

It was just like any other Sunday, but today it was Doc's Birthday. Doc was feeling a bit dejected as Morty made no acknowledgement of this milestone, as if she were totally oblivious that it was his birthday. The fact was, it was quite the opposite. This was her mischievous plot to surprise him. She had been utilizing the neighbor's kitchen to bake his cake, as not to tip him off with the familiar scent filling the house. She also told the preacher not to announce it to the congregation during the service. Conspiring with the neighbor lady and the Pastor was the easy part, compared with concealing his birthday present!

Morty dubbed this gift, God's gift to Doc, not from her. Four days prior, Morty discovered this 'gift from God' when she with her ladies' group were cleaning the church. There it was staring back at her from inside a cardboard box on the floor right inside the front door vestibule of the bell tower. It was a red puppy shivering with fear!

"What is your name, cutie?" Morty reached down and gingerly picked up the pup, looking first into his eyes, then cuddling him close to her bosom. The box was empty, not even a cloth or a blanket to keep him warm. She immediately walked back through the sanctuary searching out her friends to show them her discovery. Like showing off a new baby, the two other ladies flocked over and hovered, all wanting their turn at holding the precious bundle while talking baby talk.

"I need to find Reverend Ziglar, I'm sure he knows who this sweet little lump of coal belongs to." Morty collected her prize and set out in search of her Pastor, which didn't take long, as he was walking up the sidewalk from the Parsonage. He was just as surprised as the women and had no idea where the puppy came from. Surprisingly, the pup was weaned, it appeared to be a purebred Red Fox Labrador Retriever, which was also strange, because it was not a breed which was commonly abandoned, because of its value as a hunting dog.

Morty and Reverend Ziglar spent that afternoon plus the next day going door to door and tacking up lost puppy flyers all over town, but to no avail. No one knew of any Labrador dog owners or breeders in the community. They decided the best place to keep the pup was at the church, just in case the owner came back to retrieve him. Morty acted as caretaker, feeding and walking it while they waited, but no one came.

Saturday, she took Doc his lunch as she normally did, walking downtown with a covered basket under her arm. He was just finishing up with a patient, so she walked right in and past his receptionist Martha. Doc was sitting at his desk staring at one of the Lost Puppy flyers when she walked in.

"Hello Dear", she greeted, but her husband Doc didn't immediately respond as he was far away in thought.

"Oh hello Sweetheart! I'm sorry, you caught me daydreaming. Has anyone responded to this flyer yet?"

"No, I'm afraid not." She replied.

"I bet he's pretty cute, isn't he?" Before Morty could respond he added another comment, but much softer in tone and trailing off toward the end. "I miss not having a doggy around." His softly spoken remark didn't go unheard. Before she could respond, he capped off his thought with a stronger toned, "Well, maybe someone will claim him today." Morty stared at him for a second, then simply nodded.

"So what did you make today my darling." Doc started to peek under the cover of the basket.

"Honey would you mind eating your lunch by yourself

today? I just thought of something that I needed to do back at the church." Morty walked over and gave Doc a hug and kiss, quickly unloaded the basket, then scurried out the door. She practically ran to the church collected the puppy, walked over to the Parsonage and asked the Pastor for permission to take the puppy home. He immediately said yes.

"I suspected that you and Doc were God's intended caretakers anyway. After all he did lead you to him!" Reverend Ziglar laid one hand on the puppy's head and the other on Morty's shoulder and said a quick prayer.

When he had finished she gave the pup a kiss on his head and placed him back in his box. Morty was beaming from ear to ear practically skipping out of the church. She knew that this puppy would be the perfect addition to their family and a great companion for Doc.

She carefully hid the puppy in the pantry knowing her husband rarely went there and then snuck him outside to do his business when he was occupied on the other end of the house.

After they arrived home from church Morty went directly to the kitchen and then out the door to her neighbor's house to retrieve the cake. She finished the final configurations of the candles then went into the pantry and retrieved the puppy. She spotted the lunch basket sitting where she left it the day before and placed the pup inside, after kissing his head and shushing him she pulled the cloth over.

Doc was in his study sitting at his desk reading the Sunday paper when she walked in and placed the basket in front of him.

"Happy Birthday, my love!" Doc immediately dropped his paper and stood up.

"I thought that you forgot!"

She walked around the desk to where he was standing and threw her arms around him. "How could I forget the birthday of the one who I adore? You big dummy!" They both laughed.

"Did you bring me lunch to my study?" Doc looked at the basket sitting beside him.

"No Dear, not lunch! You might want to take a peek under the cloth."

Doc cautiously lifted a corner of the cloth which covered the basket and brought his face closer to better examine the contents. When he did, a red, wet nose poked through followed by a wet tongue which licked him in face. The doctor was not expecting this and blurted out a shriek which caused the puppy to bark. Morty immediately started laughing at their impromptu introduction. Doc stepped back with wide-eyed excitement, completely astonished at what was in front of him.

"Well, aren't you going to say hello to your new friend?" Morty knew that her husband was in shock and needed coaxing. The puppy was now up on his back two legs with front paws on the rim of the box, his tail wagging as fast as he could.

"Can I keep him?" Asked Doc, sounding like a six-year-old, as he reached over to grab his puppy. "Is this the abandoned puppy from church?"

'Yes, no one claimed him, so I thought of someone who might like a new friend."

Doc was grinning from ear to ear, as he cuddled his new friend.

"So what are you going to name him?"

Doc extended his arms to look at the puppy's eyes.

"I'm not sure yet, I need to think about that for a bit before I choose.

Honey, this is the best birthday gift that I have ever received! Thank you very much!"

The next morning Doc woke up Morty to tell her his exciting news.

"Asclepius!"

"What!?" she responded half asleep.

"Asclepius! I want to name him Asclepius, Pius for short. Asclepius, was the Greek God of medicine, and healing. What do you think?"

"I think you better go let a-slept-us out and feed him." Morty rolled over and dozed back off to sleep, barely remembering their conversation. Doc jumped up and headed downstairs anxious to share his new name choice with the pup.

From that moment on Pius and Doc were inseparable! He tucked him securely under his arm and went off to his office. After all, what better assistant could any M.D. have than the Greek God of Healing at his side. Well, that's the line that he used to explain to Morty, why he took Pius to work with him, when she showed up frantic at his office, as she couldn't find the missing pup.

Everywhere Doc went Pius was at his side, whether making house calls or seeing patients at his office, and yes Pius was present at the Hamilton house laying his head on Katheryn's chest while Doc delivered the twins. As a puppy, Doc even snuck him into church, leaving him in vestibule, where Morty found him, then picking him up after the service.

Soon everyone in North Salem knew Pius. For a few weeks Doc carried him in his satchel, but he soon outgrew that, so Doc decided to walk Pius with a leash, but that lasted only a couple of times before the leash was discarded.

It was mutually decided that neither Pius nor Doc needed to be tethered and certainly not to each other.

When Pius got a little older, Morty and Doc would drive him to their favorite getaway just West of town. Wilson's Woods was a beautiful campground full of woods, streams and deep ravines. A paradise for pups! It became much more than that. It was their retreat!

To say that Pius was an amazing K-9 would be an understatement. From day one, he came into their life as a tiny pup already weened. Soon he began to understand the Wiseheart's mannerisms, their vocabulary, everything that both Morty and Doc would say and yes, think.

Perhaps Pius's most bizarre attribute Doc would gradually discover, was his ability to understand his patients' needs and develop a certain empathy for them. Pius was a healer too, as his presence alone would lower blood pressure and ease nausea just by laying his head on the patient's abdomen.

He was comforter for the elderly and a consoler for children. But, Pius's most astounding abilities would not be discovered for years to come.

Back to the present

By the time Caddy got back to his car, the wrecker was already there, and the guy was connecting the cable. Caddy stood at the top of the hill and looked down at the man as he brushed himself off and started his trek back up to the road.

"So, you must be the drunk Doctor that owns this car." The man walked right past Caddy who stood awkwardly ready to greet him with extended hand.

"Sir, I'm not drunk, nor have I been drinking!" Caddy's cordial demeanor quickly changed to defensive.

"That's not what old lady Wilson said." The man chuckled at his comment as he pulled a few levers from the back of his truck causing the cable to start recoiling on the spool.

"I was sitting right beside her when she called you and heard nothing of the such!" The man let go of the lever and the cable stopped, which also stopped the retrieval of the car. He looked over at Caddy then spit on the ground.

"Are you calling me a liar?" Caddy was fully aware of his precarious situation but was not about to concede to this insolent stranger.

"I'm saying that she did not say that I was drunk!"

The man burst out in laughter as he walked over to Caddy. The adrenalin was now shooting into Caddy's brain as he was desperately trying to recall an evasive maneuver that he learned several years earlier in a self-defense course.

"I'm just screwen with you dude!" He then reached out his hand to shake Caddy's. "I'm Ron Goode, damn glad to meet yah! You stood your ground, that tells me what kinda person you are." This time Caddy wasn't so generous with extending his hand but did offer a snarky reply.

"I'm glad I passed your test."

Goode returned to his tow truck and resumed the gear of the pulling cable, then began to make small talk.

"What brings you through North Salem?" Goode

"A detour!" Caddy

Goode laughed. After a few seconds of uncomfortable silence Caddy decided to expand on his short reply.

"I was heading to Bloomington for a golf outing in the morning, when I was detoured off my normal route and then missed a turn. The next thing I know I'm swerving to miss a dog and here I am talking to you." Caddy paused and looked toward the warm illuminating glow of town. "You have a nice little community here."

"Yah, they're not all assholes like me." Goode laughed.

Caddy could tell that his new friend thoroughly enjoyed verbally taunting folks just to get a charge out of them and to see their reaction. So, he decided that he wasn't going to be an easy pawn in his verbal game.

"I am a doctor and the first thing they teach you in medical school is to recognize the different parts of the anatomy. You my new friend are not an 'asshole', I would say, you are more of irritant, perhaps a hemorrhoid."

For once in perhaps a very long time, Mr. Ron Goode was rendered speechless.

Caddy's car was undamaged and ready to drive, once it was retrieved from the ravine. Caddy handed Goode a credit card and sat in his car to wait. When Goode returned Caddy rolled down the window to sign the receipt and take back his card.

"It's too bad you aren't sticking around Doctor, I've got a sick little girl at home and I would trust you to look at her." Caddy signed and took back his card, then looked up at Goode.

"What are her symptoms? Isn't there a local practice that you can take her to?"

"She's got a bad fever and can't keep anything

down. I'm afraid my wife is also coming down with this too. She has the same symptoms as several folks in this town have. Caddy recalled a similar comment made earlier by Myrna Wilson. They all have been to the doctor and some the hospital and told it's just the flu. It aint the damn flu! The flu don't cause your hair to fall out. No offense, but I don't trust doctors. My wife and I don't have insurance, so I'm not sure we'll get the same treatment as those who do. Oh well, I've talked up too much of your time. Sorry about the drunk driver shit!" Caddy was no longer looking at an obnoxious uncouth brood of a man, but rather a wounded and desperate father and husband. He turned his head forward and looked through the windshield taking in a deep breath. Goode walked back toward his wrecker. Caddy exhaled, opened his car door and climbed out.

"Goode!" Caddy shouted, and he turned around.

"I'm going to follow you home!" Goode quickly perked up and acknowledged Caddy, and then climbed his wrecker. Within moments they arrived at his house.

Again, Caddy witnessed a red dog, this time sitting in the driveway, as if he were waiting for them to arrive.

He quickly pulled in behind the wrecker, threw the car in park and then jumped out. Caddy approached Goode with his arm extended pointing toward an area in the drive.

"Is that your red dog?" Caddy asked.

"What dog? My dogs are in the pen out back." Goode responded. "Thank you, Sir, for coming by! Caddy's attention went from the dog, who once again vanished from sight to the more pertinent issue, a sick child. Caddy patted Goode on the shoulder and then grabbed his arm.

"You must promise me, that if I determine that she needs to go to the hospital you must take her. Agreed?"

"Yes sir!" Goode nodded his head.

"Contrary to what you may believe, Hospitals do

not give preference to patients who have insurance." Caddy headed for the house, but before he stepped inside, he made one more survey of the yard, but no dog.

He followed Goode into a chaotic front room, did a quick introduction to a Grandmother, who was in the middle of breaking up a fight between two young sibling boys. He continued following Goode down a halfway toward a door which was hallway open. Goode stuck his head inside and in a loving tone said.

"Honey, I'm back and I brought someone to see Harley. He's a doctor."

A muttered response came from inside the room and both men entered slowly. The room was dimly lit from a lamp beside the bed. In the bed lay the mother and young daughter.

"Connie, this is Doctor Caddy. He ran his car off the road near the edge of town. After I pulled his car back on the street he agreed to stop by and take a look at Harley and you."

She pulled herself up in bed and stuffed another pillow behind her to assist her sitting forward. Looking concerned at her husband and new houseguest she mustered up a faint reply.

"Hello Doctor, it's very kind of you to stop by. No offense, but I hope that you are a better doctor than a driver." Caddy laughed at her response.

"Well, I like to think that all that money I spent on Medical school wasn't in vain. Your husband already drug me over the coals regarding my incident. He even accused me of being drunk. At his request I agreed to look at Harley, but if you feel uncomfortable with that, I understand and with respect to your decision, I'll leave. I do need the consent of both parents before I can proceed."

"Did my husband tell you he doesn't trust doctors?" Caddy looked at Goode and then back at his wife.

"Yes, he did bring that up, but that tells me how worried he must be by bringing me here."

"Please Doctor, I didn't mean to be so rude and

thankless, that's his department. I guess that if you passed his test, you must be alright. Of course, please look at our daughter. She's not getting any better, in fact her fever is getting worse and she's losing clumps of her hair."

"Please see if you can wake her while I'll wash my hands."

When Caddy returned little Harley was awake but crying. Her grandmother and two older brothers were now present, and a gallery of family members were all now trying to console her.

"Okay, everyone out, so the doctor can look at your sister!" The elder Goode stood in the doorway of a now well illuminated room and acted as traffic cop, directing the flock out of the room so that Caddy could enter. Clutching his bag, he slowly approached the five-year-old, pulled up a chair and sat down beside her. With a warm smile on his face and in a soft voice said.

"Hello Harley, I'm Doctor Cadwallader. I know, it's a silly name. My friends just call me Caddy. You can call me that too." Harley stopped crying to hear what the strange man had to say, but then retreated closer to her mom and buried her face in her side.

"It's okay Harley dear, Dr. Caddy came by to see if he can make you feel better." She pulled her face away from the safe confines of her mother's chest to take another look at the man sitting beside her.

"Your mommy is right. I'm going to try and find out why you're not feeling well and see if I can make you better. You can help me if you want. Caddy was without his stethoscope or a thermometer but would have to make do with his natural senses. He spotted a toy medical kit in the corner of the room, walked over and pulled out a plastic stethoscope. "When we are done looking at you, you can help me take a look at your mom. Would you like that?" The little girl wiped away the tears from her eyes and nodded. Caddy moved from the chair to the bed to get closer to Harley. He looked over the stethoscope and then placed the tips in his ears, handing the rest of the device to Harley. He instructed her to hold the bell tight against her mother's chest. Caddy involved her with everything and even though she was extremely weak, she enjoyed being involved in making his exam a lot easier.

Caddy concluded his thorough physical assessment of Harley and Connie before asking them a salvo of questions.

"You both show all the signs of a virus. That is, except for the loss of hair and the longevity of the illness. I can't determine the illness without more tests. If several people in town are suffering with the exact same thing, that tells me that whatever it is, it's contagious. You say that you've been keeping cold cloths on her head and giving her Children's Ibuprofen, but her fever is not subsiding. On the nightstand beside her bed was a thermometer inside a glass. Caddy looked at Ron and pointed at the glass. "What has been their temperature readings? For two days, both have been a steady 102 degrees. Connie spoke. Harley should show signs of getting better by now."

Caddy interjected his professional opinion to Ron and Connie. "Because you don't have a regular pediatrician or family doctor you need to take her to the closest ER and have their doctors look at her. I'll write a note, suggesting that they admit you both, at least until her fever is gone. I'll recommend they draw blood and take urine samples, perhaps run additional tests if determined necessary." Both parents looked at each other, then nodded their heads in agreement.

Caddy excused himself and went to the kitchen to start writing his narrative, leaving the family to get ready for their trip to the hospital. After finishing writing his instructions to the ER doctor, he returned to room to find Harley alone and out of bed. She had made her way over to the window and appeared to be staring out at something. Connie and Ron were right behind Caddy as he entered the room.

"Harley sweetheart what are you looking at?" Connie asked in a concerned motherly voice. She turned around with a big smile on her face and said.

"It's just my friend the red dog again mommy." Hearing that, Caddy rushed over to the window.

"Don't bother Doc, she's been seeing this make-believe 'red dog' for several days, I think her fever's making her delirious.

"He's real daddy! Just like the people said." Ron shook his head and responded, "Crazy people in this town, believing folklore as fact." Ron leaned over and picked up his daughter, but not before Caddy quietly interjected in Ron's ear.

"No disrespect, but I saw him too. However, that's not important right now. You need to get her and your wife to the hospital." Caddy looked out the window to a vacant dark yard.

"Just like what people said?" Harley's statement seared into Caddy's brain as he followed the Goode's out to their car.

"I can't thank you enough, Doctor! What do I owe you?"

"You owe me nothing!" Caddy responded. "We are all square."

Ron reached in his pocket and pulled out the credit card receipt from earlier and ripped it in two.

"This is the least I can do for your troubles!" He then turned his attention to helping his wife and daughter into the car and securing them in. When done, he walked around to the driver's side, waved to his boys and mother on the front porch and climbed in. Caddy walked closer to the car and motioned for him to roll down his window.

"Sometimes, our Lord works in mysterious ways! I've decided to stay tonight at 'Pearl Street Bed and Breakfast', so if you need anything, please don't hesitate to call me. In fact, I would love to hear from you later as to what the ER Doctors find." Caddy handed Ron his card with his cell phone, and the Goode car pulled away.

When Caddy returned to the bed and breakfast Myrna had his dinner waiting. To his surprise a lone place setting was poised on a white tableclothed dining room table. A bell on the front door jingled signaling his arrival. He sat his bag down and within seconds Myrna appeared carrying a steaming plate and a pitcher of ice-tea. She motioned for him to sit in front of the setting, and he obliged. Caddy devoured the home cooked meal of porkchops, mashed potatoes and corn, in minutes. When he finished his last bite and before he set his fork down, Myrna appeared again, this time with a slice of cherry pie and a cup of coffee. She leaned over and sat it in front of him. He smiled, commented on how delicious it looked and invited her to join him.

"Ms. Wilson would you do me the honor of accompanying me? I'm very curious to hear all about that red dog."

"I will, but we're going to need the whole pot of coffee!" She wheeled around and exited back to the kitchen but returned a few minutes later with the pot and another cup for herself.

July 1949

Record heat temperatures were predicted by the morning paper, but that didn't deter the daily routines of the community of North Salem. The town was a bustle with farmers in grain trucks delivering harvested wheat to the grain elevator. Mainstreet was a gathering spot for boys, mostly huddled in front of the grocery, waiting for the recently emptied farm trucks to collect them and take them back to the wheat fields to bale straw, from the stems separated from the threshing. Most of the men in town were employed either by the Grain Elevator or by the Sawmill and thus most of Doctor Wiseheart's mid-summer visits came from both businesses. Usually, he would see patients with heat exhaustion or deep lacerations due to carelessness. For other ailments, summer was a slow time for and today would prove to be no different for Doctor Wiseheart's office. Doc decided that he and Pius would walk down to the post office and collect his mail.

"Come on Pius, let's go see if we got a response from Emmerson."

The Emmerson that Doc was referring to was good friend and renowned Doctor, L. Emmerson Philips of the Mayo Clinic. They became close friends after meeting at a Polio seminar in New York City in 1942. They connected after Wiseheart found Philips wallet wedged between the cushion of a sofa in the hotel lounge.

Normally when the doctors corresponded, it was regarding the topic of hunting or fishing trips, but recently their letters revolved around a concept that Philips presented while they were on a fishing trip in Michigan. The topic of discussion had extreme interest for Doc, mostly because of its medical implications, especially regarding treatment. The topic was the treatment of Rheumatoid Arthritis, a painful disease that was crippling many throughout the United States and all over the world. North Salem wasn't exempt from this disease, as several of Wiseheart's patients suffered from its residual symptoms too. As a physician Doc felt helpless because he couldn't ease their agonizing pain.

Dr. Philips was leading a team of physicians at Mayo treating Arthritis patients of all ages with a wonder drug called Cortisone, which they administered through periodic injections. Since their fishing trip, Philips had sent Wiseheart several articles and medical books related to this treatment. Wiseheart was intrigued with its initial success and wanted to offer this treatment to his patients.

Before he could do so, he needed permission from the Mayo Clinic and just as important, he needed access to the vaccine. Doc and Pius's trip to the Post office hopefully would retrieve the letter from Dr. Philips which would solve this dilemma.

It was his lucky day; the letter did arrive. Doc was so excited that he didn't wait to get back to the office. He tore into the letter immediately and even read the highlights to Pius.

"My Dear friend Oscar, it seems that I have convinced Mayo that the clinic here in Rochester wasn't receiving enough arthritis subjects to treat, thus jeopardizing an accurate study. I suggested that they needed to expand their territory, perhaps several miles from this facility." Doc had captured Pius's full attention, so he read on. "The Board of Regents left the selection of the satellite location completely to my discretion, so the transition to your office should prove to be very efficient." The letter went on to explain more details in depth including Dr. Philips' explanation on how he was also able to have the pharmaceutical laboratory ship the experimental cortisone direct to Doc's office. As part of the agreement Doc was to provide detailed documentation to Mayo of his treatments, along with his patient's medical history and reactions to the injections.

It wasn't hard for Doc to find volunteers to take cortisone shots as his patients, like most Americans were desperate for any kind of relief. Within a couple of weeks, the relief serum began arriving. News travels fast in a small community and soon arthritic patients were coming from several miles away including other states to receive Doc Wiseheart's wonder injection.

Doc never turned anyone away and as a result the daily lines to receive the relief shot grew and grew. Soon the lab was shipping him more cortisone than it was shipping to the Mayo Clinic.

Doc Wiseheart would never take appointment.

Whenever or whoever would show up at his office or his house, he would treat them. When the news got out about his successful arthritis treatments, ailing people showed up in masses. The additional sufferers mixing in with his normal patients put a strain on his practice, but not for long. Prioritizing patients according to their severity of illness or suffering was not a problem as Pius was on the job. Unexplainably, he began patrolling the lines and would sit next to the patient who most urgently required Doc's attention. When Doc concluded an exam, he would walk his patient out and collect the next

His patients quickly adapted to this irregular procedure and accepted Pius's unbiased selection.

It was several years before cortisone injections were universally allowed as a common treatment for arthritis, but Doc's documentation of his treatments went a long way toward helping the Mayo Clinic receive approval for this experimental treatment.

Caddy took a sip of his coffee while intently watching Myrna pour her own cup.

"So, you saw the red dog! Wow, you are one lucky man, Dr. Wells. You now belong to a rare fraternity of individuals who've actually witnessed that K-9 apparition. I'm sad to say that elite group doesn't include me, and I've lived in North Salem for sixty-three years. Hell, I even live in Doc Wisehearts house now and I have never as much as seen a picture of his dog."

"Okay, so wait a minute, Ms. Wilson. You just said 'apparition'. Just to be clear, I never implied that the red dog that I encountered was some sort of a spirit or ghost." Caddy laughed sarcastically. "Please be careful how you phrase that. I would prefer that my name not be used to legitimize some kind of crazy ghost story. That nonsense could taint my reputation. All I stated was that I swerved to miss a red dog, perhaps a Labrador and that I followed him here to your place. I guess, for the record, I did see him again standing in the Goode's driveway. But that still doesn't imply that he's a spirit and not just some stray."

"He's not a stray! Her voice sharpened as if she were insulted by Caddy. "If it were a stray, it would be around all of the time and begging for food. Besides, despite that, it's been quite a while. That's not the first time someone has spotted a red lab around my house or on my porch." She turned her head away and lowered her voice, finishing her thought. "It's not the first time it's vanished right before our eyes either! The dog did once live here, you know. Pius is his name. He was the former resident, Doc Wiseheart's dog."

"I guess that I'm a little excited and to be truthful, a little nervous too. Usually when he shows up, it's either right before or during an unpleasant event. The red dog hasn't been spotted in years until recently, two weeks ago by a couple of residents in town and now you. I was a little suspect of the honesty of the two locals who claimed to have spotted him on different occasions, but your encounter, a complete stranger, confirms in my mind that Pius is out and about." Ms. Wilson paused a moment as if she were debating whether to continue this particular conversation with this doctor of medicine that she just met, or take it in a totally new direction. She felt compelled to stay the course despite her unease of his opinion of her sanity, and proceeded on.

"I am jealous Caddy, I have never actually seen him. I do, however, feel his presence from time to time, and have even felt his breath on my arm, usually when I'm reading a book in the den. My first night in this house after moving in twenty-some years ago I was awakened in the middle of the night by a jarring. It felt like something just jumped on my bed. This occurrence usually happens only once in a blue-moon, but the last few weeks it's been happening with more frequency. It doesn't really frighten me anymore, but I find it hard to fall back to sleep, because it feels like he's staring at me."

Caddy looked Myrna in the eyes while she reflected, trying to analyze whether she was being truthful or merely sensationalizing for her guest.

"Well, I'm not so sure how rare red dog sightings are. Just in my short time here in North Salem I met another person who's seen him as well. That person is little Miss Harley Goode and she and her mother are not doing so well. In fact, I'm waiting to hear from Ron, he promised me that he would call me once they found out what the ER doctors discovered.

You mentioned earlier that several people were sick in town, do you know their symptoms?" Caddy switched his conversation from the illusive red dog to a subject that he was more educated on, illness.

"Yah, lots of folks around here are sick. They've been sick and they're not getting better. That is, unless they die!" She pressed her hands together and looked up at the ceiling.

"Rest in peace, Grace Bowen!" Myrna paused a moment, then realized that her guest may need some further clarification.

"This virus, or whatever it is taking a toll on us, especially the elderly. Grace was the first victim. She passed quietly at home, telling her family not to worry about her because Pius the dog was at her side. There are two more residents around her age in the hospital. I'm told that Oscar Mount probably won't make it through the night." She sighed and then continued.

"Oh, that poor little dear child, Harley. I had no idea that she or her mother was sick too.

"You realize, Dr. Wells, if it were not for that dog, you would not have connected with Ron Goode, and would not have called on his sick wife and child. If you weren't able to persuade him to take them to the hospital, oh Lord, that would have been tragic." Caddy didn't hesitate to respond to what she had just said.

"That's probably a bit over dramatic, Myrna. I'm sure that he would have taken them regardless of my intervening. He just wanted to get my professional opinion to confirm his thoughts.

"Tell me Mrs. Wilson, to your knowledge, is everyone being told by their respective physicians that their illness is viral?"

Myrna nodded her head and just as she began to speak, Caddy's phone rang.

"Hey Doc, it's Goode."

"Yes, Ron…"

"You told me to call you. Well, they are keeping Connie and Harley overnight, just to get fluids back in them. They'll release them in the morning. It seems they don't give a damn about your letter. They're not going to run tests; they say it's just a virus."

"I was afraid of that!" Caddy turned his head away from the phone and commented in disgust.

"I am sorry Ron, I should have come along with you. You need to contact your family physician in the morning and…"

"Nope, I appreciate you looking at my wife and daughter earlier, but my commitment to you is over! I'm not obligated to take orders from you or any of these bastards here at this dump! As soon as they disconnect the tubes from them in the morning, we're out of here." That was Ron's final remark as the connection ceased.

"Damn, what am I saying? He told me earlier that they didn't have a family Doctor." Caddy shook his head in disgust. "It's not a damn virus!

Myrna, where is that hospital from here?"

"About ten miles from here, due East. I can drive you, if you want." Offered Myrna.

"That's not necessary, but thanks." Caddy replied.

He scooted himself away from the table and walked over to the door.

"Will my bag be alright there until I return?"

"Of course! Good luck, Doctor!"

She gave a quick hand gesture wave to Caddy as he stormed out the door, then collected his dishes.

September 1949

Doc was enjoying breakfast with Pius who was securely tucked under the table at Kisner's Café. The 'No pets allowed' sign didn't apply to Wiseheart's medical assistant, the towns favorite 4-legged son. Once or twice a week the boys would sneak out and give Morty a break from fixing them their first meal of the day.

All of the sudden, Pius jumped up and began to bark, interrupting everyone in the café.

"Pius, be still!" Doc immediately scolded him for his rare public outburst, but that only seemed to ignite his behavior more. After circling the table a few times, he darted toward the door. Before Doc or anyone could respond to let him out, a customer entered giving him the opportunity to-make-a-rapid-exit. Suddenly, a loud BOOM followed by a wave of seismic vibrations inundated the café.

The large plate-glass windows trembled violently as if they we going to burst, and the china rattled like windchimes announcing a storm. A mere second seemed like an eternity, but once their brains processed the situation it sent impulse signals causing a simultaneous reaction. And the reaction was Hysteria! Soon everyone in Kisner's Café followed the lead of Pius by crashing through the door and out into the street.

There they were joined by patrons of every downtown business. Complete chaos consumed all as everyone was running in different directions trying to locate the source of the explosion. The whistle from the top of the Water Tower started to wail, compelling the people on the street to move back to the sidewalk in anticipation of the arrival of the firetruck. This whistle summoned the North Salem volunteer Fire Department and it could be heard for miles. The firetruck was not the first emergency vehicle to storm the street. It was the town

Marshal's squad car with lights and sirens intensely raging. Marshal Dennis Hope had heard the explosion too and was now on the way to find the source. The Marshal spotted Doc amongst the crowd and threw on his brakes, he rolled his window down and motioned Doc over to his car.

"Jump in, Doc!" He obliged, and they sped off.

"What's going on Dennis?"

"I don't know yet, but whatever it is, I got an awful feeling I'm gonna need your assistance."

As soon as they passed the buildings of the downtown business district, ground zero of the explosion revealed itself. Marshal Hope made a hard left and barreled down one of the residential streets pointing them in the direction of the billowing red smoke.

"It's got to be the grain elevator!" Hope yelled over the blare of the siren, to his passenger Doc and he nodded back in agreement. The sidewalks were full of alarmed residents. The elderly stood dazed and confused, while young children were clinging to their mothers or grandmothers. Few men were home at that time of the day, but the ones that were ran valiantly toward the direction of the explosion. As the squad car drew closer to the end of the street and the source of the paroxysm, the scene became grimmer. Houses were completely engulfed in flames, some blown completely from the foundations and there was debris everywhere. And there he was!

"Stop Dennis, there's Pius!" Doc pointed to his dog, who was at the front door of one of the houses consumed by fire. Before the car could completely stop Pius ran toward the street, turned around and darted back at full speed jumping through the front window. Seconds later Doc was running up the walk leading to the house after his dog. "Pius'! He yelled as he leaned through the shattered window. He yelled again despite choking on existing smoke. Marshal Hope now stood beside him and also began yelling, but he was calling out the name of the resident.

"Mrs Hadley!

"Doc, I think I see something, I'm going in." The Marshal turned his head away long enough to fill his lungs with clean air then proceeded to step through the opening. Just then a distorted silhouette appeared through the dark smoke. It was Pius and he struggling to drag something. That 'something' turned out to be Mrs. Hadley. Marshal Hope took over for Pius. He reached down and grabbed the 85-year-old unconscious women under her arms, pulling her up. In one motion he moved her past his lanky frame and positioned her over his shoulders.

He decided it was best to return to the gaping void where the window used to be, then try to struggle with getting the door open. He was blinded by the thick smoke and the flesh on his face was burning. These were minor sufferings compared to the pain and convulsing due to the incapacity to take in oxygen. Despite this, he forged ahead making it to the opening and handed her over the sill to Doc. From there Doc carried her to the yard and began resuscitating her. Marshal Hope crawled through the opening followed by Pius. He stumbled to the yard and then collapsed to his knees gagging and choking to regain his breath. Pius didn't stick around but was on to the next house. The cavalry arrived in the form of the fire department, and town volunteers both on foot and in vehicles were now on the scene. Marshal Hope regained his strength, jumped to his feet and ran to the street to direct the chaos. Seconds later firehoses were connected to a hydrant and then dragged across the yard, past Doc and Mrs. Hadley. There were multiple dwellings on fire and only one pumper truck, so starting at the Hadley house was as good as any.

They speculated that the source of the explosion was the grain elevator, but they could not get near it because of the intense heat. As far as the other streets they could only imagine that they were in the same condition as one that they were on.

The south end of town was an inferno and Marshal Hope and the Fire Chief immediately recognized the real threat of them not being able to contain it and losing the whole town.

They were emphatically undermanned, and they needed help. The Chief radioed to all the towns in the county for their help while Marshal Hope contacted the State Police.

Amidst the chaos, Doc was able to revive Mrs.

Hadley but she needed hospitalization for which an arriving neighbor lady graciously offered to drive her there. He feared that there would many others, so he immediately began shouting out to the arriving crowd for volunteers with cars to be on the ready, as the town had no ambulance service.

"Where was Pius?" Doc's focus immediately changed as he sensed that wherever his dog was, there would be someone in destress. He grabbed the arm of a stout teenage farm boy helping to drag a firehose.

"I need your help, son!" The boy did not hesitate, he fell in behind Doc and they urgently began treading through the smoke-filled streets searching for his dog and any casualties he may have found.

The penetrating sounds of sirens from the additional arriving firetrucks were merely a white noise now. Each arriving fire department took a different street. There were two operations underway, search and rescue and fire extinguishing. Marshal Hope, and the growing group of volunteers were going from house to house, opening the front door and yelling inside. If the door was locked, he would kick it in. Doc and the boy were heading toward what was presumed to be ground zero of the explosion, the town grain elevator, all the time searching for Pius.

It didn't take them long to find him. As soon as they came to the end of the residential street where it connected with the street leading to the elevator, there he was. Pius was lying beside something in the middle of the street and Doc immediately realized that that something was a body. He ran over and knelt beside Pius whose head was resting on the victim's chest.

Once Doc started his evaluation Pius jumped up and was off again. The body was burned beyond recognition, but miraculously still breathing and semi-conscious. Doc immediately stopped the boy from getting any closer, but instead directed him to get help and find someone to drive him to the hospital. The victim was trying to speak but struggling. "Ammonia Railcar."

"Lie still. Don't try to talk, we'll get you to the

hospital." Doc was at a disadvantage because he was without his instrument bag. He realized that there wasn't much in his bag which could help this person except for a vial of morphine which he remembered he had recently put there.

Doc couldn't help this poor man other than to hold his hand and console him while waiting for help.

The street they were on paralleled the railroad tracks which lead to and past the grain elevator. The grain elevator was the economic heart, or pulse of the farming community, and the railroad was the artery or the lifeline. Farmers would haul their grain to the elevator and sell it. The elevator would in turn store the commodity and, at some point, resell it to large grain mills. Transporting the large volume of grain to the mills was the job of the train.

The elevator would load the railcars and the train would take the grain to mills in either Indianapolis or Chicago. The elevator would also serve as the distributor for farm products or supplies, such as livestock feed supplements or fertilizer. Today, the viable heart of the community was lost, destroyed by an explosive force.

From his knees Doc stared down the smoke-filled street lined with railcars, which were billowing flames, to what was left of a large structure, all engulfed in a transient inferno. If the scene wasn't dire enough, Doc spotted more bodies strewn across yards and streets. It appeared the explosion catapulted them into the air before depositing them like ragdolls. As he started to rise, he was startled by a hand grabbing his shoulder from behind. It was a fireman, and standing behind him was the boy, they were carrying a stretcher. Doc told the suffering man that help had arrived, and they would soon be transporting him to the hospital. He helped lift the man onto the stretcher and gave them some instructions. Before they exited the area, the Fireman turned and urgently waved down an arriving tanker truck to their location.

Immediately, men began departing the vehicle, clinging to hoses as they debarked. The hoses were connected to the tank and they immediately began dispersing water.

Doc headed toward the next casualty, still brooding that he didn't have his medical bag. Pius must have sensed his concern because just as Doc arrived at the victim, Pius showed up carrying his bag in his mouth.

Pius however didn't stop, he ran past Doc, crossed the street to a smoldering structure, that was the remnants of a home, intact just 20 minutes earlier. Doc stood up and addressed his Dog. "Pius! Where are you going, I'm right here!"

Pius dropped the bag at the end of the walk in front of where the front porch once was. Not hesitating a bit, he looked toward Doc, growled a bark, then gingerly walked up and onto the rubble.

Doc turned his attention back to the crumpled body lying next to his feet, he knelt, placed his fingers under his chin and applied pressure. To confirm that procedure, he laid his ear on his chest, but after a few seconds Doc raised his hand and placed it over the eyes of the victim and said a quick prayer.

Unlike the first victim he attended to which was unrecognizable due to severe facial burns, this young man he did recognize and knew well. In fact, he delivered him into this world nineteen years prior.

Relaying the news of his tragic death to his parents later would be an undertaking that would haunt him for his remaining years.

Like a sprinter out of the starting blocks Doc ran hard toward his Labrador. He now realized that Pius knew that the young man had passed and that he sensed someone still living in the rubble of the imploded house.

As with most small towns in America, everyone knows everyone else, on top of that, many of the town folks are related. If you happen to be the town doctor, you not only know everyone, you also know every private and personal thing about them. Even more so than the town's church pastors. Things were no different in this town or with this doctor. At least once in his 30 plus year career, Doc Wiseheart had been in every home in this town. He has treated not only every citizen of this town but also for most rural families for several miles in circumference, as well.

He has prescribed treatment for just about every ailment under the sun however, medical school and years of small-town practice experience could not prepare Doc for this horrific war-like scene. For the rest of the citizens, volunteers and victims this event would haunt them for the rest of their lives.

Pius was barking profusely standing on the smoldering rubble and staring down at the floor at an area of protruding wood beams.

Doc motioned for the arriving fire crew to spray down the area, but he didn't wait for them to complete this action, as he grabbed his bag and went directly to join Pius.

"What did you find, Boy?" Doc crawled up next to Pius and with the spray from water hoses now coming down on them he peered down into a crevasse between the wood beams to discover what caught Pius's attention.

"Please help us." A weak voice came resonating up through the debris.

"I hear you Mrs. Campbell! We'll get you out." Doc could not see down the dark chamber but could hear the woman's faint cry for help. Seconds later there was another cry, but this time it wasn't Mrs. Campbell, it was a child's voice. Standing over his shoulder now were two fireman who had just arrived in time to hear the cries. They immediately started pulling away debris from the opening, but their efforts only made the situation worse.

"Stop! You're knocking loose rubble into the hole and on top of them." Doc's instruction was moot, as the firemen realized what they were doing and immediately stopped.

"We need to tunnel in from the side. It's not just Mrs. Campbell, but it sounds like she's got her grandson with her, too."

Pius figured out the solution before Doc and the

men. He had found a void off to the side of the rubble and was digging to expose a larger opening. Well, large enough for him to squeeze through.

"We need a tractor to pull away the heavy trusses, or we'll never get to them!" One of the firemen shouted after assessing Pius's entrance, fortunately an onlooker overheard his request. "My farm is close, I'm going to run home and get my Allis-Chalmers WD45."

Before he finished his sentence, Pius was already in the hole and crawling toward the Campbell's.

Pius managed to make his way to Mrs. Campbell and her grandson, Sam. They were terrified and pinned in the rubble, but miraculously only had minor injuries, as was revealed later.

Pius nudged his nose over to the young lad enough that despite the dark he could feel his breath. Sam in turn stretched out to his limit, pressing his cheek against the cold and wet snout. The actions of the dog not only calmed the boy down, but it soothed his grandmother beside him too.

Soon the farmer returned with his tractor along with a host of help from the community. The result of their efforts freed the grandmother and child. While the gang was working to exhume them, Doc moved down the street to the next victims. His findings, however, were not good, as sadly he acted more as a Coroner than a physician.

After several grueling hours of mental and physical exertion, the adrenaline of the Volunteers began to wear off, and exhaustion took its place. By early evening, the town's water tower was completely drained, and the firetrucks had to resort to retrieving water to fill their tanks from a river three miles away.

Luckily, and despite the inconvenience of transporting the water, all the fires were extinguished before ten o'clock p.m., but the search for victims continued and lasted through the night.

Dawn finally came, and the light exposed the dire and utter destruction of the south side of the town. There were smoldering piles of rubble where houses once stood, a void in the skyline where a grain elevator building once filled. The most grimly surreal sight exposed by the sunlight, was the yards adorned with rows of individual white sheets.

The streets were now absent of firefighters, but replaced with mourners, reporters, and State Police Investigators.

Within a couple of days, the State investigators were able to confirm what most of the town had already surmised. The cause of the devastating explosion and fires was a tanker railcar filled with anhydrous ammonia parked at the grain elevator. Anhydrous ammonia was rapidly growing as the premier form of fertilizer used by farmers throughout the Midwest, but it was very volatile. The grain elevator also served as the distributor of this fertilizer to the farmers.

What the investigators could not conclude was how, what, or who ignited this unconventional bomb. All but one of the employees of the elevator was killed instantly by the explosion. The lone survivor just happened to be a block away walking downtown to pick up supplies from the hardware store. He had just turned around after hearing a loud hissing sound coming from back at the elevator. Seconds later a railcar parked adjacent to the main building lifted off the tracks, then everything turned white. Before the man could react, he too became airborne, hit by a sonic force of fire and energy.

Like most of the town, Doc was exhausted, both mentally and physically, it was a struggle for him to carry on his doctor responsibilities. He wasn't the only one affected in the Wiseheart house, either, Morty spent most of her day praying across the street at the church. For days Pius would not even leave the confines of his house. He did not eat or drink. He was deeply depressed and acted ashamed as if he had some culpability in this tragic event.

Caddy was on his way to the county hospital. He had a feeling gnawing at his gut that the Goode's were not suffering from a virus, but something different. He wasn't leaving North Salem until he had confirmation, one way or the other. Golf in the morning with his buddies was the last thing on his mind.

Caddy didn't want to bother the Goodes anymore. It was clear that Ron was agitated with the whole turn of events and probably blamed him for the hospital trip in the first place. He noticed a couple of things in his quick exam of Connie and Harley that were inconsistent with a virus and he felt obligated to discuss his findings with the staff physician at the hospital. He recognized that the note he gave

Ron to pass along lacked professionalism, but it was the best he could do at the time. Thus, his scribblings were probably not taken seriously and didn't motivate them to issue further tests. Even so, he was agitated that the E.R. doctors were quick to judgment without consideration given to other possible causes.

Caddy soon arrived at his destination. He pulled into the emergency parking lot, parked, departed the car, and urgently walked through the twin automatic sliding doors toward the medical welcoming committee poised behind the glass partition.

"Good evening ladies, my name is Doctor Cadwallader Wells! When he or she is available, may I speak with the lead physician on duty tonight?" Caddy had his identification card in his hand and presented it for all interested to verify.

"That would be Doctor Black, I think he's available. Just a moment." She turned around and gave a nod in the direction of one of the nurses in the back prompting her to jump up and scurry away.

Soon she returned, towing a tall silver haired man in white lab-coat, presumed to be the E.R. doctor. She momentarily stopped and pointed across the room toward Caddy, then resumed in the direction of her post while the man continued walking around the partition.

"I'm Doctor James Black, how may I help you?" The emergency room doctor stood within a few feet from Caddy with an inquisitive look on his face. Caddy extended his hand to make his acquaintance and announce his name. Doctor Black recoiled a bit and nodded his head as if he were already familiar with Caddy.

"Thank you so much for taking a moment to see me. I won't take up much of your valuable time, but I wanted to chat with you regarding Mrs. Goode and her daughter. I believe they were admitted a few hours earlier and are possibly still here. I convinced her husband, Ron, to take them to the hospital after I did a quick improvised diagnosis at their house."

"I sent along a note, but I realize it was a bit

unconventional and probably didn't receive much consideration by you or your staff. Well, actually, that's why I'm here. I don't believe that what they are suffering from is a virus."

Doctor Black cleared his throat and then crossed his arms.

"I did read your note, Dr. Wells. Come with me!"

Caddy followed the E.R. doctor into an empty observation room. Once across the threshold, he doubled back and closed the door.

"I'm sure that you are all too familiar with the privacy laws wherever it is that you practice, so our conversation here will be quick and succinct and after you leave, I'll forget that we even spoke." Clearly agitated by Caddy's visit, Doctor Black took in a long breath and exhaled slowly as if to calm his nerves. Then he continued.

"Doctor Wells, if you only knew how many patients a week I've seen from North Salem in the past three months, and all suffering from the same symptoms." He shook his head.

"Do you also realize how many of those folks have no health insurance? I know the Goode's need additional tests. They all do!"

"Maybe where you practice, money is no object and most individuals are fully insured, but not around here.

Many of the people I see have to decide which is more important, feeding their family or doing more than the bare minimum for their health recovery."

"I don't know why I'm sharing this, but twice I reported this outbreak to the county Board of Health, and once to the state. So far, either agency has not done a thing. No investigation. Nothing! They tell me they'll get to it when they can. It's not a priority until at least three people die and the cause of death cannot be explained. Budget constraints!"

"Doctor Wells, we don't have the resources of a major metropolitan community, but we do what we can. I am certainly aware that skin lesions and scarring of the retina are not symptoms associated with the common virus, but the patients I treat don't. To speculate without blood testing on the multiple patients I've seen would be wrong! More importantly, to needlessly panic a small community would be irresponsible and immoral! I simply tell them the truth, that I'm unsure of their illness, could be a virus, or it could be something else. I then try to prescribe what they can afford to make them more comfortable."

"You must excuse me now. I need to attend to my job." Caddy said nothing through Doctor Black's verbal diatribe and just let him vent, but it was now his turn to speak.

"I didn't intend to be critical and I apologize for overstepping my boundaries, I merely felt an obligation to help the Goode's, a family which I just met. A passion for the Hippocratic Oath, you understand!" Doctor Black, who started to leave the office, stopped, nodded his head and sighed.

"Thanks for reminding me of the Oath, Doctor Wells! I didn't intend to unload on you. I realize that you had no idea of the circumstances here." Doctor

Black softened his tone but stopped just short of apologizing. He then excited the room. Caddy followed him out into the hall but stood motionless watching him until he disappeared down the long sterile white corridor. He needed a moment to absorb the nuances of the E.R. doctor's lecture, but his moment was over, and it was time to return to the bed-and-breakfast.

During the lonely, late night drive back his brain was consumed with thoughts and scenarios, none of which involved golf. Today's series of events changed Caddy's focus entirely.

There was some sort of epidemic going on in this small town and nothing was being done to find out the cause, let alone the cure. "Budget constraints. They'll get to it when they have a chance!" Those statements infuriated Caddy. "If I just had one day in the community!" He thought. "Perhaps I'll take this route on my return trip to Evanston. I could drop by, check on the Goode's, maybe a few others and collect a few blood samples. Monday's are normally clerical, no procedures, but I'll call the hospital to confirm my schedule. Doctor Hanson can cover checking on my patients if needed." Caddy was pleased that he had this worked out in his mind.

As he pulled up in front of the house, a final thought crossed his mind. As he exited the car, he blurted it out, confident that no one would hear. "Budget constraints my ass! All it takes is just a little bit of time and compassion."

"I got lots of time and compassion!" The unexpected response came from the dark front porch. As he walked closer, he could see Mrs. Wilson sitting on the porch swing.

"Am I in trouble Mom, for staying out past my curfew?" Caddy laughed, but apparently Myrna didn't see the humor and didn't respond. Finally, the awkward silence was broken as Caddy was now standing, smiling and staring down at her.

"How is Connie and little Harley?"

"They are stable. Being treated now for dehydration, as if it were a virus."

"Did you talk with the doctor on duty?"

"Yes, I did. Caddy replied. "I know it's late now and I'll be leaving early in the morning, but I would like to chat with you about what is going on with the illnesses here. I would like to stop back by on my way home. Perhaps spend another night and half the following day."

"Doctor, you're always welcome here and I will be at your beck and call when you return!"

"Thank you, Myrna! So, I'm going to turn in, but I will see you tomorrow night." Caddy walked on, heading inside to his room.

"I'll have coffee and cinnamon rolls waiting for you in the pantry at six." He smiled at her and replied as the screen door shut behind him. "Thank you, Mrs. Wilson!"

Caddy had the whole upstairs to himself, so waiting to share the bathroom with other residents was not an issue. There was even a plastic cup with his name on it waiting for him beside the sink which he obligingly filled with tap water and took to his room, after brushing his teeth. Soon he sank into the deep mattress of an antique four-poster bed and fell into a deep sleep.

Suddenly disrupted sleep is something that one never becomes accustomed to, even to a doctor who's constantly on call.

This doctor was no different, and the shock of the sudden waking was compounded by the unfamiliar environment he was now in. Harsh, pulsating frequencies of boisterous diatonic shrillness shattered the placid silence of the night. This chaotic sound managed to diminish the rustling and shaking of the bed he lay in. Caddy immediately rose in fear only to be encountered by the dog jumping on his bed and barking profusely. Once the dog had his attention he moved to the nightstand and knocked over his monikered cup spilling the water onto the floor. The dog then commenced toward the door and exited the room. Caddy whose adrenalin had peaked jumped to the floor and trailed the dog into the hall. Only a couple of seconds separated their departure, but when he passed through the door to the hall, the dog was gone. The night lights illumined the corridor and the staircase, at least well enough to see a shape, but there was nothing. Not even a shadow!

He stood motionless for a few seconds to listen for any sound, then a few more to consider his options. Justly, he decided to return to his bed.

Morning came fast, but there was no more sleep for Caddy. He showered, collected his belongings and headed downstairs. Precious coffee awaited him in the kitchen and the aroma of the freshly baked cinnamon rolls led him there. Beside the pot, there was a note from Mrs. Wilson.

"Good Moring Doctor, help yourself to coffee and rolls. I am off to church. Have a safe trip, a fun day golfing with your friends and I will see you upon your return. I look forward to our talk!"

~ Your friend, Myrna.

Caddy filled his cup, grabbed a roll and headed out the door.

Morty filled Doc's coffee cup and kissed him on top of his head as he sat motionless staring at his dog lying by the door.

"Look at you two sorry broods!" Morty orated.

Doc looked up at his wife, and then over at Pius.

"Pius, your Mother has a point here! It's been nearly a month since the tragedy and you and I, along with many in the town have just been going through the motions of life, not living life. This in itself is a tragedy!" Pius looked up at his Master with discernment in his eyes. Doc continued his thoughtful speech, with confidence that Pius would grasp everything he would say.

"We have no answers to why sometimes really bad things happen in life. But it is written in the scriptures that God never gives us more than we can handle.

North Salem cannot mourn forever, as the grief will surely kill the rest of us. It's time we start rebuilding what was destroyed by the explosion and fire. I'm not just talking about the buildings; I'm also talking about our souls! We need to rebuild the life in this town!"

When Doc finished, Pius jumped up and belted out a dynamic bark, as if to announce to the world that he received his orders and was now ready to carry out his assignment!

Doc swallowed the last few ounces of java from his cup, scooted his chair away from the table, wiped his mouth with a napkin and stood up.

"Well Pius, are you ready?"

Doc gave Morty a kiss, and he and Pius were out the door.

Doc had an idea on how to bring life back to the town, but he knew that when the idea would come, he would need to get the town behind it. In order to do this, he needed a way to convey his idea. He required a forum, of a captive audience of townsfolk. Two obvious forums which immediately came to mind were the church's and the tavern. He was now heading to the parsonages to sell the pastors of three churches on his idea. Hopefully this would engage them to convey it and ask for support from their congregations on Sunday.

North Salem like most small towns in America, were very strong in faith and that got them through the tragedy.

All three churches held prayer vigils around the clock for seven days after. His strategy was to spend the morning converting the clergy, in the afternoon he would venture down to the local watering hole, which would be open then and he would chat with his subordinates there.

Doc was received with open arms from the pastors of all three denominations. The tavern took a couple of rounds of beer to completely capture their attention, but they finally came around too.

His opening spiel had already been rehearsed on Pius back at his kitchen table, so it was delivered confidently and left his audience ready to hear his idea to bring the town out of post-mortem and back into the living.

"We need to have a community celebration! A parade! Festivities for all. Singing. Dancing. Music. We'll devote it to those lost in the explosion. We'll block the streets off from automobiles. I've already thought of a name. We'll call it Old Fashion Days! You know, covered wagons, horses and all that."

At first there was an awkward silence from his audience. They stared through him as if they were not sure of his sincerity. Slowly they came around and soon they were even interjecting with their own ideas.

Doc asked for volunteers to form various committees and there was no shortage of offers. His idea was set in motion. A week later, a unanimous choice of Labor Day weekend was selected to be the date of the inaugural event. Labor Day was two months away and there was much work to be done, but the task the good Doctor set out to do was accomplished. He prescribed an antidote to cure the town from depression and it was working.

The town was on the mend, but the horrific visions of that tragic day would be cast forever into the dark caverns of the minds of those who were within the city limits. Nightmares would haunt those who witnessed the carnage for the rest of their lives. From that point on, the lore of this small Indiana town of six hundred would be centered around 'the day the town exploded'!

Caddy opened his car door and climbed in. Balancing his coffee in one hand, he inserted the key and turned. Music from his satellite station blared, startling him to react quickly to adjust the volume to zero. Something else was not right, he sensed. He went to engage the P to D and the shift knob was froze. It was also too quiet. There was no engine hum, he realized. Caddy reached up and advanced the key forward again, this time a blaring radio couldn't squelch out the most annoying sound known to automobile owners. The sound of clicking which usually indicates a dead battery, or in this case, a battery with just enough juice to play the radio but not enough to turn over the engine.

"What the @#*@!" Caddy bellowed a string of profanities while he pounded his steering wheel with his palms. The calm and measured demeanor usually associated with a surgeon was immediately replaced by the quick-tempered actions of a fraternity brother realizing he was about to miss a tee time with his fellow brothers.

Still mumbling to himself he reached between his legs and pulled the hood latch. As he was about to exit, two paws lunged up and knocked against the driver's side window, nearly scaring the excrement from him and causing him to forget about his predicament. "It's that damn dog again!"

Caddy ascended from the car and walked around to the front, but as he was reaching for the hood, familiar barking rang out. Letting out a sigh, he spun around to see the dog running at a fast clip in the middle of the street toward downtown. Suddenly the dog stopped, turned and darted toward a church. It was several blocks away, but it appeared as if he ran right through the doors.

Seconds later, 'tat, tat, tat'! The distance muffled the sound to some degree, but he recognized it to be gunshots and immediately he started walking toward it. Then people came pouring through the doors and into the street. Caddy pulled his phone from his pocket and began running. "911, what's your emergency?" The emergency operator inquired.

"There appears to be a shooting in North Salem and it's in a church on main street, downtown!" Caddy was gasping for air as he ran and talked simultaneously.

"What is your name sir?" "My name is Dr. Cadwallader Wells! I heard shots being fired followed by people exiting the structure. I'm running toward the scene. I'm also unfamiliar with this town, so I cannot give you an address and I don't even know what church it is."

Caddy was almost there. In the background was the sound of sirens. "Please remain on the line!" The operator requested. "I've arrived! I can't talk any longer, but I won't disconnect!" He slipped the phone in his shirt pocket, as he was now amongst the parishioners.

Surprisingly, the scene was not hysterical! Many were grief stricken and crying, most were praying! Some of the elderly sat on the curb with their arms around each other. On his approach, Caddy passed mothers scurrying their children away, but other families remained just a few yards from the front door.

Everyone was visibly shaken, but they were calm and at peace. He gave a quick scan of the crowd, and no one appeared to be injured or hurt. "What's going on?" Caddy cried out. "Our pastor has been shot!" Several voices responded in unison. "They're still in there! We are waiting for the EMT's!" Others screamed!

"I'm a doctor, does anyone here need my assistance?"

"Please, go and try to help them!" A woman in a choir gown reached out and grabbed his hand, leading him in through the front door. As soon as he stepped across the threshold, a thought rushed his brain. "Was this Mrs. Wilson's church?"

As soon as they were on the inside, Caddy pulled the woman behind him and pointed for her to go back outside, for which she refused! "It's okay, the ushers have him! They have the shooter!" she clarified. The vestibule was empty but echoed multiple loud voices from farther inside. They walked urgently through the second row of glass dividing doors and they were now inside the sanctuary.

A carpeted aisle separated rows of wooden pews that led to the nave. To one side of the altar, on the floor, three men had a woman pinned.

The captive was writhing from side to side and yelling profanities. On the other side of the altar lay a white robed man, presumed to be the pastor in a pool of blood. Knelt beside a woman was frantically working on him.

Caddy ran toward the victim. Upon arrival he recognized the woman. It was Myrna! She was covered in blood, but not all of it was the Pastor's. He reached down and laid his hands on her shoulders causing her to flinch and look up. Her eyes were deep with fear and filled with tears that were now spilling over onto her cheeks. She acknowledged Caddy by touching his arm, stood up and then collapsed. As Caddy caught her, he caught something else in hid periphery, a faint image standing next to the pipe organ. Caddy thought he saw the dog. After he stretched Wilson out horizontally on the floor, he turned to quickly look again, and the image was gone.

A quick examination of Myrna Wilson revealed that she had a puncture wound in her lower abdomen, and the bleeding was minimal. He then crawled over to the pastor and felt his neck for a pulse, and then gently pushed back his eyelids to observe his pupils. Caddy shook his head and returned his attention to Myrna.

Down the aisle lumbered the town marshal with gun drawn. Behind him, EMT's cautiously entered the sanctuary and immediately crouched behind the last row of pews. Once the officer realized the imminent threat from the shooter was gone, he exchanged his gun for cuffs and yelled to the EMT's that it was safe to advance.

Within seconds the emergency responders were hovering over him. A few feet away the screaming and demonic bellowing from the women increased in volume as the marshal cuffed her.

Upon their arrival, Caddy announced that he was a physician and they immediately began assisting him in treating Mrs. Wilson and preparing her for an ambulance trip to the county hospital.

Caddy borrowed a stethoscope to confirm the Pastors passing and the coroner was summoned.

With the help of smelling salts, Myrna began regaining consciousness, and right before they lifted her onto the gurney she spoke. "God sent Pius to save my life. Today he saved many lives!" During her escorted exit she raised up from the constraints of the gurney and looked in the direction of her assailant, now sitting motionless leaning against the pulpit.

"I forgive you Sarah and God will forgive you too!" With that, Wilson motioned her male lorries to continue and they fulfilled their responsibility by delivering her to the ambulance.

Soon the sanctuary was filled with state and county police. The alleged murderer known now as Sarah was still sitting, but her incessant profanity screaming had ceased.

A female officer approached her with a notepad, and she began rocking back and forth and mumbling to herself

Golf with his buddies was not in the cards this year for Caddy. At this moment, it was the farthest thing from his mind. That is until his phone rang. When Caddy saw who was calling, he let it ring into voice mail, but responded with a text. "I'm sorry! I'm not going to be able to make our tee-time. I can't talk now, I'll call later!"

"Who was Sarah? Why did she shoot Mrs. Wilson

and kill the Pastor? How did Pius the dog save the life of Mrs. Wilson and the other parishioners?" Caddy's head was spinning with these questions and there were no immediate answers coming from the chaotic scene inside the church.

The officer in charge asked him some basic questions and took down his contact info, but because he wasn't an eyewitness, he wasn't detained. Caddy walked out of the church to find the sidewalk and street had doubled with bystanders and now a few news reporters with crews joined the fray. Immediately, all noise ceased, and every eye was upon him. A news reporter rushed toward him, but before he could reach Caddy, a voice from the audience cried out, "Who are you"?

The town folk immediately recognized that Caddy wasn't one of them. Relevant or not, the reporter picked up on that inquiry from the congregated gallery and responded accordingly. "Sir, can you tell us your name and where you are from?" Before Caddy could respond, another voice from the gallery replied. "He's a doctor! Didn't you hear him say that earlier?" Caddy looked the reporter in the eye.

"I'm Doctor Cadwallader Wells, from Evanston, Illinois. I'm just passing through this town and staying at the Pearl Street bed and breakfast. I heard the shots and ran down here to help!"

Caddy anticipated the reporter's questions and wanted to direct the conversation to a quick conclusion.

He continued to walk forward through the crowd.

"Doctor, can you confirm that the pastor was shot and killed?" The reporter walked along side Caddy continuing to ask him questions. "I really can't offer you any more information than what I have already."

Caddy wasn't compelled to drive to Bloomington, but instead got in his car, which ironically started without issue. His destination was back over to the hospital to which he was only the night before with the Goode's. This time it was to check on his recently acquired lodging

By chance it was Doctor Black on duty and he

just happened to be at the E.R. admittance desk when Caddy came through the sliding glass door.

"Let me guess, you are here to check on Mrs. Wilson!"

Caddy looking puzzled, smiled and nodded at Doctor Black's greeting. He continued.

"I released the Goode's hours ago, and I'm fairly sure that you aren't looking for a job." Doctor Black looked down at his chart in his hands and chuckled.

"This is interesting, I'm looking at her admittance notes here, and it states that a doctor Wells treated her on the scene. That would be you, right?" He turned and motioned Caddy to follow him. "Sign in here doctor and follow me on back to ICU. We first need to get you cleared through security."

Caddy did as instructed and followed him through the swinging door, past the emergency rooms, down the corridor to intensive care. Caddy caught up beside Doctor Black and they walked together the rest of the way to her room.

"Ms. Wilson is in the second room to the left.

Luckily, the bullet entered and exited her without damaging any internal organs or breaking any bones.

Her wound was clean. You can say that it was a miracle! Vitals are normal and thanks to you she didn't lose a lot of blood. We'll probably release her soon. I believe her brother's with her now."

Two sheriffs stood guard in front of the door. Doctor Black introduced Caddy, and after a quick review of his driver's license both doctors entered the room.

"Mrs. Wilson, I've got someone here who wants to see you."

"Cadwallader!" Myrna shrieked, as she was surprised to see him, but she immediately grimaced in pain as a result of her elevated voice. Caddy rushed past her nurse and a man to get to her bedside. Myrna labored to take in a breath. "I am so sorry! I spoiled your golf game."

"Nonsense!" Caddy quickly replied, while reaching out and clutching her arm. "Shush! I play golf all the time, I'm a Doctor! What I don't get to do is interact with a hero!"

Caddy gave her his warmest bedside smile and then turned around to look at the man that he walked by moments before.

The man was standing in soiled denim overalls and sporting a Pioneer Seed Corn hat. The brim nearly covered his eyes.

"Doctor Wells, this is my brother, Randy." Myrna motioned for him to come closer, but Caddy instead initiated the gesture by reaching out his hand and shuffling his way. They clasped hands in a non-sanctimonious salutation, followed by a verbal monotone response of *'nice to meet you'*. Doctor Black decided to make his exodus at the conclusion of their quick introduction.

"Well Doctor, I've got other patients to see, so this is where I bid you fond farewell." He turned away from Caddy and looked directly at Myrna. "By-the-way, not all doctors spend their days playing golf! Some practice medicine!" Doctor

Black didn't pass up the opportunity to take a jab at his counterpart. "Mrs. Wilson, you are one lucky woman! Hospital policy regarding gunshot wounds insist you stay as our guest tonight, but if no issues come up overnight you are free to check out in the morning.

I signed your release papers along with a simple pain prescription and instruction to follow up with your personal doctor in a week. You also experienced a lot of drama today! A life changing tragedy. Not just that you were shot, you witnessed a murder. More importantly you witnessed the senseless death of a friend, your Pastor. I highly recommend that you seek professional counseling, at least on the short term. I will jot down a few names for you to call. I also suggest that your brother and or other family members stay with you for a few days." The doctor looked at her brother, Randy. "I don't think that this tragedy has fully sank into your sister yet." He looked back at Myrna. "Your community will need lots of prayers, and strong leadership. I don't know all of the details of this senseless act of violence, but I do know that God spared you today. He must have big plans for you!"

With that parting statemen, Doctor Black left the room.

"So, Myrna, I strongly agree with Doctor Black about seeking counseling. You must not keep today's events bottled up inside. Community group counselling, I would recommend. I witnessed your incredible courage today!

You could be a big help to others in your congregation by giving them strength! I know that you have been talking to the police off and on all day, mostly answering questions, but if you just want to talk, I'm a good listener. I assume events like this are not a common occurrence in North Salem." Caddy smiled and looked at her brother for his input.

"She claims that her friend the invisible dog saved her life. You should tell her not to bring that up with her counselor, they'll lock her up!" He rolled his eyes and shook his head. "Damn ghost story!"

Myrna grimaced in anger and turned her head away from her brother.

"I saw him to", Randy! In fact, the dog encouraged me to follow him to the church moments before the shooting! The whole reason I'm here and staying at your sister's place is because of that dog. Did you say his name is Pius, Myrna?"

Myrna immediately turned her head back around and raised up relying on the support of her arms. A gleam replaced the grimace on her expression. The grimace didn't go far as it now consumed her brother Randy.

"What kind of doctor are you, a 'nutjob' psychiatrist?" Randy wasn't prepared to hear Caddy's testament. In fact, he was shocked!

"Whack-job! Both of you are whack-jobs!" Randy muttered his retort, then walked over and kissed his sister on her forehead and said that he'd see her in the morning.

As soon as he walked through the door and out of their sight, Caddy looked at Myrna and spoke.

"Well at least we have that in common!" Myrna laughed.

"I'm sorry about Randy! Actually, several people think that I am a 'Whacko'. What you said, did you really mean it? Did you really see Pius?"

"You know that I did!" She looked him in the eye and nodded.

"Tell me Myrna, who was that lady and why did she shoot you and your Pastor?

I also want to know everything about Pius, but that can wait. I've decided to hang around North Salem for a few days. That is if you'd have me as a guest at your place."

"What about golfing with your buddies?"

"What about it? They'll just have to tee up without me." Caddy smiled

"Sarah Carmichael killed James!" Myrna struggled a bit saying his name and then hesitated. For the first time she showed some emotion. She took a deep breath before continuing. "Pastor James Clark. You talked about counseling earlier, Pastor Clark was counseling Sarah. Actually, he was counseling both of us. We are both grieving widows. She more recently. She interpreted his counseling as love, but when he rejected her, she blamed me." Myrna stopped and broke down. Caddy handed her a tissue, leaned over and gave her a hug.

"You don't need to continue!" He patted her on the back. "You need to get some sleep."

His advice went unheeded and she continued.

"She intended to kill me! After she shot James several times in the chest she whirled around and pointed the gun at my head. Pius, out of nowhere, lunged on her back. She fell forward and the gun went off striking me in the stomach." She began to sob harder! Caddy knew that he needed to leave, but the doctor in him needed to prescribe something to help Mrs. Wilson sleep. So, he summonsed a nurse and requested that she ask Dr. Black for a sedative. Caddy also wanted to them to draw blood to test while she was there, because of his concern over her dizzy spell the other night. The hospital doctor, Black consensually agreed with Caddy's request for the sedative, but again denied the blood work, just as he did with the Goode child. Caddy was puzzled by Black's response, but out of respect said nothing. He realized that it was time for him to make his exit.

It seemed like just an ordinary day in 1952, but not so, as fate would have it. For on this day Doc would receive a mysterious package in the mail that would change his life, the lives of the town and hundreds of others for many miles in circumference would benefit from its contents.

Every morning, Monday through Friday Pius and Doc would take a 15-minute break to walk down to the Post Office, collect their mail, chat with the Postmaster and then return to his office on South Broadway Street. On occasion, he would receive a package, which was generally medical supplies that would be too large to fit in the mailbox. When that would occur, the Postmaster would leave him a note to collect his parcel at the window. However, Doc would never get the opportunity to read the note and follow the directions as McGowan the Postmaster would always be waiting to greet Pius and him when they opened the bell triggered door.

"It's Doc and his Dog", he would shout. "I've got a package!" He sang out in dramatic fashion. Then he would proceed to tell him where it came from and render a guess as to the contents, hoping that Doc would open the package to confirm his speculation.

This day McGowen was a bit more animated as the Doctor's shoebox sized package was from Rochester, Minnesota. More specifically, a place called the Mayo Clinic in Rochester.

The word Clinic barely left the mouth of McGowen before Doc reached across the counter and snatched the package away from him. Doc was so focused on the package that he didn't hear the Postmaster rambling in the background and left without checking his regular mailbox.

"What the Hell is Emmerson sending me from

the Clinic?" Doc muttered to himself as he left the government premises.

"Hey, where are you going? Aren't you going to open it?!" McGowen shouted, but to no avail.

Doc rushed back to his office, bypassed his receptionist Betty, and went straight to his private room in the back. It wasn't that he received a package, as he gets several a week for his practice. But, getting something from an old friend from the Mayo Clinic, that a whole different ballgame. On top of the contents was a folded, handwritten letter.

My dear and old friend Oscar,

I missed you this year at the alumni dinner in Louisville. It was as droll as ever, but thanks to your absence the Kentucky School of Medicine has a new and gracious coordination host for next year. Your gratitude is not necessary, but I'll relish it just the same. I trust you'll find it in your heart to forgive me for writing your name in, on your behalf. For the record, I believe we are now even, for the amateurish prank you levied on me with my suture supply. Have fun next year! Haha!

Well, on to business, accompanying this letter in

the box, you will find 15 vials of an experimental medication serum that Mayo's been administering to severe arthritic patients. This truly is a wonder drug, and in a short period of time we have had much success. The blend of medicine used in the serum along with the recommended injection rate is written on a card underneath the glass vials.

I am infuriated to inform you that our research will soon terminate, as a result of a disgruntled intern leaking our research methods to the media. Much of the early research has been conducted on animals, injections administered by veterinarians to livestock.

As you know, this is a very common practice. However, much of the public is unaware of this. Certainly, the public is not privy to the facts.

This disgruntled individual has secretly been sensationalizing this practice to the journalist scribes portraying it as cruel and baseless for collection of data.

Mayo is very concerned about the negative publicity and how it could potentially devastate all funding at the clinic, that they are willing to abort this particular project.

Mayo may be conceding, I, my friend, am not! I do, however, need assistance. Assistance, that is, with no connection to Mayo. Thus, I am writing this letter to seek your help! I need willing patients for treatment, and I need a physician who can administer and record the results. Your unpretentious midwestern town could provide the perfect setting to continue our research discreetly on consenting adults without compromising integrity. I promise you that there have been absolutely no issues or side effects with either humans or animals! What we have seen is almost instantaneous relief from the horrific pain inflicted by Rheumatoid Arthritis after each injection!

What we don't know is what the long-term effects are. We also need to ascertain; this is a cure or just temporary relief?

Supply is virtually unlimited! We have several

thousand vials in a warehouse here in Rochester and an infinite source across the border in Canada.

I will be waiting for your favorable response!

Yours truly,

Emerson.

Dr. Emerson Philips

Research and development

Mayo Clinic

Pius sat attentively, staring at Doc as he read the letter. Even though he read to himself, Pius appeared to understand every intended nuance that was scribed by his friend. Doc set the letter on the desk picked up the box and pulled out a vial.

"Seems that we have a wonder drug of sorts here Pius!" He held the vile up so that the sunlight from the window illuminated the liquid. "Arthritis. So many suffer! How wonderful would it be if we could ease their pain?" Doc looked away from the vial and into the brown eyes of his friend who was sitting and listening to every word he said.

"What do you say we get started? Are you ready to make some house calls Pius?"

"Woof!" An enthusiastic Pius scurried over to the credenza, jumped up with his front paws and grabbed Doc's bag with his mouth. He then delivered it directly to his master. Doc put some vials in his bag along with Dr. Philip's recommended dosage, grabbed some syringes and they were out the door and on their way. Doc knew that he would have no trouble with finding elderly volunteers to try the concoction. Several were desperate for relief from the pain.

Immediately he decided to start with three of his most pain afflicted, debilitated patients. If he could see results, mainly pain relief in a day or two, he would expand the treatments by three individuals a day.

Without direction from Doc, Pius knew exactly where they needed to go, and Doc fell in behind him.

"Where are you taking me Boy?" Without stopping,

Pius turned his head and looked back at Doc as if to say, keep up! It was uncanny how mentally connected Doc and Pius were. The first one who Doc thought of was Rosie Davenport and that was exactly where they were headed. Rosie had an advanced form of rheumatoid arthritis along with diabetes, which kept her bedridden most of the time. There had been countless visits to her house to see the tear filled eyes of her husband, Frank begging him for anything to ease her pain. These traumatic events kept Doc awake at night praying for some, or any, medical breakthrough which could offer help. Perhaps this was the answer to his prayers.

Frank answered the door and was a bit, as it wasn't Doc's normal day to visit.

"Hello Doc, I wasn't expecting you! You must have told me, and I forgot."

"No Frank, nothing has changed with our schedule. I apologize for just dropping by like this, but I may have something that might help Rosie. I couldn't wait for my regular visit to tell you about this. How's she doing today?"

"She's awake, would you like to ask her yourself?" Doc smiled and nodded, but not to be left out, Pius barked.

Rosie was awake and the four of them gathered around her bed as Doc took her vitals. Once he finished, he began to explain why he was there and about the package he received from the Mayo Clinic. He could see the excitement in their eyes as he read portions of Emerson's letter, but cautioned them about getting their hopes up because it was still an experimental drug. When he was done with his bedside presentation, he didn't need to ask if she would like to try an injection. Both Rosie and Frank simultaneously requested that he administer her a shot.

He did, and then he and Pius were off to the next house.

Indeed, it was a miracle, Doc's prayers were answered! The next day he returned to the Davenport's to find Rosie sitting up at the kitchen table. A week later she answered the door. This miracle injection had returned life to her and she and her husband were beyond grateful!

He experienced the same miraculous results with the two other arthritic patients, so keeping to his plan he shared the treatment with other inflicted individuals.

The news spread like wildfire about his miracle drug, and after a few weeks his clientele grew from beyond the limits of North Salem and even Indiana. Arthritis sufferers were showing up in droves. Doc Wiseheart never turned anyone away and he only charged each individual what they could afford. Mayo's warehouse soon became empty of serum, so Doc set up direct shipments from Canada.

Doc kept a journal with the progress of each patient he saw that day. Beside each name, he jotted, 'No side effects!' Once a week, he would mail his findings to Doctor Emerson. Occasionally, Emerson would, ask Doc to fluctuate dosages or monitor other patient related activities.

Something was compelling Caddy to hang around this small town. Perhaps it was the unknown sickness that was afflicting its citizens. Or maybe it was the drama of the church shooting. Or, just maybe, it was that damn dog. Conceivably, it was all three.

But certainly, the most haunting was Pius the dog! Was he a myth, an apparition, or just a stray dog who just shows up at the right time and no one notices but a select few? A select few that he now has the honor of being part of.

Caddy headed back from the hospital to an empty bed-and-breakfast, but not an empty town! The streets were filled with people, with a large crowd centered in front of the church. Camera crews from the local television stations were mingling through the mob looking to interview that one individual who would shed some insight into the incident. Yellow crime scene tape fluttered in the breeze in front of the house of worship, creating a surreal image of despair. This circus like spectacle didn't fit this Midwest small town persona!

Caddy had to alter his route and detour around this to get back to the bed-and-breakfast.

Myrna instructed Caddy to help himself to anything in the kitchen and pantry, so he did just that. It was late afternoon and he had not eaten since the day before. Having free reign to comfort food prepared by one of the best cooks in this town would be a dream come true for most bachelors.

However, in Caddy's case he felt some reservation knowing that he was a guest of the cook and she was lying in a hospital bed after nearly losing her life. He did find a bowl of fried chicken, to which he helped himself to that relieved his hunger pains. After he cleaned up his mess in the kitchen, he poured himself an iced tea and walked out to the front porch. Caddy sat down on a wooden rocker and from his position he was able to view the commotion downtown.

Curiosity was calling his name and coercing him to be a part of the crowd, but better judgment prevailed, and he remained, viewing the fray from afar.

The crowd dissipated as the evening grew. Caddy turned his attention to the orange sun as it disappeared behind the trees to the west.

For better than an hour Caddy had been ignoring the buzzing of calls and texts on his phone. His golf buddies that knew his location, had now seen the breaking news reports of the church shooting on the clubhouse TV's and they were all trying to contact him. Caddy realized he needed to respond, but first he would retrieve his laptop from his car. He also needed to attend to business back at his practice and could do this while group texting his golf buddies.

The sun was down, the porch was dark, and the house was empty. The faint glow of the street lights now illuminated a vacant town. A somber scene fitting the conclusion of a dramatically morbid day.

This doctor was tired, so after he responded to the montage of texts and emails, he decided to turn in. Caddy went inside and locked the door behind him.

The house was pitch black, but he didn't want to turn on any light downstairs. So, he used the light from his phone to show him a path to the staircase.

Once upstairs, he turned on the light switch to the hall, bathroom and of course his bedroom. All he could switch off before retreating to his bed.

Sleep came quick for Caddy and he did not wake until the morning sun hit his eyelids beaming through the east window. There was something waiting for him at the end of the bed. He sat up immediately and then jumped completely out of bed. The item itself didn't startle him, as he had one very similar. It's how it got there that alarmed him! There would be no way that a leather medical bag would go unnoticed, especially to a doctor. Caddy slowly approached the bag as if it were a sleeping wild animal.

When he got within arm's reach, he poked the side. It didn't explode, so he marked a bomb off his list and proceeded to pick it up. Caddy gingerly picked up the case for a closer inspection. A silver nameplate below the leather strap handles and beside the zipper said Wiseheart.

He pulled up the silver tab and began to unzip.

"Stethoscope, thermometer oral, thermometer rectal, a worn reflex hammer, pretty basic stuff for a small-town doctor." As if someone was taking notes, Caddy mumbled off the inventory as he came to it. Then he came upon an item that most doctors would omit from their bag. He then held it up to the light as if her were inspecting a priceless piece of jewelry. "A dog collar complete with tags!" Caddy smiled and nodded as if his find suddenly made sense. He muttered one more word as he read the tag. "Pius."

"Did you bring me your master's bag, Pius?" Caddy looked around the room and projecting his voice as if he wanted to make sure that the dog heard him. "You knew that I was without mine, didn't you boy?"

Immediately after his verbal banter a rush of provocative thoughts flooded his brain. Including the idea that he was in a coma from his accident and this was all a dream. Or, for whatever reason, he had suddenly and completely relinquished his sanity. Caddy then began to question his actions and thoughts.

"After all, I am a highly educated individual! A respected Physician! My life is sustained by logic and none of this I'm now experiencing is remotely reasonable." Caddy continued his analysis.

"Still, why am I here? What is compelling me to stay? Enough of me, what is causing all the illness in town? Damn it, I'm doctor. I care for the sick and I'm here in this small town, so I shall offer my help!" Caddy's self-justification was concluded, and so was the process of brushing his teeth.

How the good Doctor Wiseheart's medical bag got on the bed was irrelevant now. Doctor Wells needed to borrow the contents, so he picked it up and headed downstairs.

The town once again was a buzz! The sidewalks were full and again people were spilling over into the street. Caddy walked over to his car parallel the curb, opened the passenger side door and placed the bag on the seat. Standing and staring at the throng downtown he pulled out his phone and looked up a recent number.

"Ron, this is Doctor Wells."

"I know who it is! Caddy?"

"I wanted to call to see how Connie and Harley were doing. I'm still in town and could run by to check on her if you'd like."

"Why? Do you need some extra cash? You're in luck. They haven't been poked or prodded yet today."

"No sir, there's no charge! Is everything okay?" Caddy wasn't expecting his sarcastic retort.

"I'm sorry!" Mr. Goode's tone changed. "They are still the same. Nothing has changed! Our little girl is still very sick. Please do, come on over." Caddy could feel the father's pain and anxiety over the cell phone.

Caddy knew that in order to do a proper analysis he would need to draw blood from the two and have it tested. But he also knew that he didn't have the appropriate blood-draw equipment or more importantly, a medical lab at his disposal. Their doctor and local hospital made it clear that blood tests would not be considered.

Caddy grabbed the stethoscope and thermometer from the case beside him, exited his car and walked up to the Goode's door. Ron greeted him at the door and escorted him back to his daughter's room where both Connie and Harley were sharing a bed.

Caddy walked over to the bed and Connie acknowledged him with a feeble smile, but Harley did not wake. Caddy gave a brief salutation with Ron chiming in showing his support. He asked her a couple of questions and told her that he would check out Harley first, before proceeding to her.

Both of their pulses were strong and seemingly unchanged since he saw them before, but both were still running fevers. They seemed to have less energy, and their skin color was a paler amber. Harley was more swollen and the lesions on her face and hands were redder. Connie said she was still losing hair, and both were barely eating or drinking.

"Mr. and Mrs. Goode, I realize that I am not your doctor and before a couple of days ago, I was a complete stranger. Connie, I believe that what you and Harley have is not a virus. If you were my patient, I would order a blood draw to know for sure and to help me diagnose and treat. I don't have the ability to draw your blood as of yet, or a medical lab to analyze it. I was planning on spending today making myself available to your community, giving similar exams as I gave you. I have connections with a Laboratory in Chicago that I can ship samples to, but it will take a couple of days before I can receive blood drawing equipment and vials. My advice to you is to immediately seek another medical practice to get their opinion on this!"

"Doctor Wells, we have no insurance! No other practice will take us! That's why we visit the E.R. because they can't turn us away.

They also won't use any additional resources, like the lab.

So, we get the bare minimum to suffice the law.

In other words, it may take me awhile to pay you, even if you did have what you need to draw their blood."

"No place in the Hippocratic Oath does it mention the patient's ability to have health insurance. You need not worry about my compensation! Both of us need to focus on getting your wife and daughter well!'

Buzz' Buzz' Caddy's phone lit up; with an area code he didn't recognize.

"Hello."

"Cadwallader, this is Myrna. Myrna Wilson from the bed-and-breakfast."

"Oh, hello Myrna. My son just brought me home from the hospital. Your stuff was still here, but you were not, so I wanted to let you know I was back. I also wanted to apologize for my absence and getting you caught up in this mess! Most of all I wanted to let you know that I am deeply indebted to you for stopping my bleeding and saving my life. I can't thank you enough!"

"I'm glad you are home Myrna. You are one very lucky lady! However, you do not need to apologize to me for anything!"

"There's a reason that I'm here and thanks to that dog of yours, I think that I am beginning to understand what that reason may be. I'm about to leave the Goode's residence and head your way, I'll explain when I get there.

"Oh, one more thing. If it's okay, I will be staying with you a few days longer."

"It's more than okay! I am very excited and I'm sure Pius will be too!" Myrna laughed and then ended the call.

A few minutes later Caddy joined Myrna at their favorite gathering place, the front porch. After pulling his car in front of the house and parking it in his newly acquired spot, he walked up the steps and sat down next to her. She invited him to sit next to her by patting the mahogany planks of the porch swing.

"How are you feeling, Myrna?"

"Well I won't be bailing any hay for a few days, but at least I'm here! It's going to take a lot more than a piece of lead in the belly of this old bird to put me out of commission." She laughed.

"I admire your attitude! What kind of medication did they prescribe?"

"Oh, they sent me home with all kind of drugs for pain and infection. Of course, I started to take a pain pill, filled my glass with water from the tap, turned my back for a second and the glass was knocked over. I forgot that something doesn't want me to drink water from the faucets around here. I can't remember the last time that I actually drank water from the tap. Weird stuff, all the time!"

"Did you take your pill?"

"Oh yes, my bottled water never spills!" Myrna shook her head.

"Okay, well I'll add that to the long list of strange phenomena that's occurring in this town. Right now, I want to talk to you. Actually, I want to request your help in figuring out what's causing all of the illness in this town. I want to offer my service to anyone who wishes to receive it. No one knows me, but they know you.

You can take me to the homes of the shut-ins, and you can also offer me a space here in your home for those wanting to visit me for a check-up. Initially, I need place to draw blood. I also need a base address to receive blood drawing and medical supplies and ship the blood to a laboratory in Chicago."

"Damn right I'll help! I always wanted to be a medical assistant!" Myrna chuckled with excitement but cringed a bit when her animation caused her pain from the wound in her abdomen.

"I've got a better idea for a base/office. Instead of the bed-and-breakfast, how about Doctor Wiseheart's old office downtown? I own the building and it's been vacant for years! It just needs a little cleaning and moving some boxes out of the way and it's all set." What kind of blood drawing stuff do you need? I bet our veterinarian, Doc Power has all the needles and tubes you need. That would save days in shipping! Let's go see him right now!"

"Wow! You are a hell of an assistant, Mrs. Wilson! Let's go visit the vet and then show me to my office!"

"I'll call my two teenage grandchildren to meet us at the Wiseheart office, they can help clean up!"

With that, Caddy rose to his feet turned and reached out his hand to assist Myrna to her feet. Their plan was set in motion!

Indeed, veterinarian Power did have blood extracting needles, cannula tubes, and germ-killing alcohol. Plenty of initial supplies to perform immediate phlebotomy procedures until Caddy could receive a shipment from Chicago. Venipuncture of animals is a very similar procedure to humans, just with more of an assortment of needles. Power was very excited to help as he was also seeing the effects of this outbreak of illness in his town. He didn't charge for the supplies. His only condition was that he be a part of the team.

He insisted on helping with administering the

procedure as well as rounding up patients. He would prove to be a tremendous ally!

Within 30 minutes of Caddy and Myrna's introduction to Doc Power, the three were off to the Goode's to collect blood from Connie and Harley. The total procedure took only a few minutes. It couldn't have gone any smoother if it were drawn in a hospital. They packed the blood-filled vials in a cooler of ice, stopped by the butcher, replaced with dry ice then headed to the nearest FedEx to have them shipped.

Myrna and her crew of grandchildren got the Wiseheart office back in shape to receive patients. Caddy phoned his office back in Evanston to inform them of the additional time he would be away.

Taking blood from all who were sick turned out to be a monumental task, so they condensed it to a random and diversified number and treated them all as best they could.

Some had to be transported to the hospital for treatment. Doctor Cadwallader in conjunction with Doctor Black was able to prescribe some medications to relieve symptoms as best they could. Myrna Wilson was able to bring the town's churches together to fund the medicines of those in the community who couldn't afford them.

Within a week, Caddy had seen virtually every sick individual in town. Virtually every household had at least one person who was suffering.

At this juncture, all Caddy could do was wait for the lab results. However, by the end of the week, he recognized one interesting fact. All who suffered from this sickness lived within the limits of this town.

Doctors throughout Indiana and the Midwest, frustrated that they couldn't help their patients, were now sending them to see Doctor Oscar Wiseheart. As a collateral result literally hundreds of physicians, medical professors and journalists descended on North Salem, all seeking the recipe for Doc's relief drug. This onslaught was causing much concern for Doc!

Doc was entrusted with this experimental drug by his good friend representing the Mayo Clinic, but his convictions were much deeper now than when Doctor Phillips introduced him to it. He felt that perhaps God chose him with this gift to help the sick. Not to prosper! Not to benefit financially! Not to share with the masses who would certainly market this drug in a self-serving way. Doctor Emerson Phillips was thrilled with all of the data he was receiving from his partner. Its positive success so far more than exceeded his expectations.

Doc promised Emerson that he would not divulge anything regarding the recipe and makeup of the drug or where or who he obtained it from. He wasn't some foolhardy country doctor, Doc realized that it was only a matter of time before someone would trace the main ingredient back to Canada and subsequently figure out the medicinal cocktail. He was amazed that as of yet no one had made the connection, the Canadian medical journals had been reporting this healing discovery for a few years.

Today, Doc would mail his friend Emerson what would turn out to be his final monthly patient report, not knowing that before it had a chance to reach him, he would suffer a massive heart attack and die at his desk at Mayo.

Eight days later, Doc would be in Rochester, Minnesota delivering his eulogy. He had written and delivered a beautiful tribute, but there was no mention of their recent medical venture. Doc commented on his friend's intellectual gift, as well as his unambiguous fortitude.

He spoke of Emerson's commitment to research and his contributions to finding a cure for diseases such as Rheumatoid Arthritis. Doc concluded his homage with, 'Someday the world would recognize Doctor Emerson Phillips achievements the same as his friends and family gathered here today'.

Doc wasn't sure what Emerson did with all of the data that was sent him. He suspected they were probably in a locked file cabinet now archived forever in the bowels of the clinic. Doc's daily records were not so thorough. For his patient's receiving injections, he just wrote, 'Gave shot'. He didn't even keep a record or journal of the scads of folks who just showed up.

He held on to the original card detailing the formula and dosage which Emerson sent him and stuck it in the bottom of his leather medical bag.

Morty was waiting at the train station to collect her husband. Pius sat patiently at her side. The thing with the Wiseheart's, they never used a leash on Pius. There was no need! He never strayed, never wandered and was generally always at their side. The good folks from North Salem were used to seeing this and never thought there was anything out of the ordinary. However, that was not the case when they ventured outside of the city limits. Today, he accompanied Morty to the big city of Indianapolis and to Union Station. Pius received several looks, hugs from smiling children and of course, a rude comment or two. Doc and Morty expected this response and were not bothered.

The train rolled up to the concrete platform and expelled a large volume of steam. It was at that point that Pius rose to his feet and began to wag his tail in exhilaration.

"Who's here Pius?" Teased Morty.

The side doors to the iron horse all opened at once and the passengers began to exit. Pius and Morty's eyes were fixated on each individual who stepped through the threshold until they saw who they were looking for.

"There he is!" Morty informed Pius, as she waved for Doc's attention and proceeded toward his direction. Doc acknowledged and then collected his bag.

Pius was used to waiting his turn until the Wiseheart had finished sharing their affection. He waited patiently while Doc planted a big kiss on Morty's lips that seemed to last for hours. Once they separated, he knew that it was his turn!

"How's my boy?" Pius knew that that was code for, 'jump up and get a big hug!'

"Pigeons!" 'The town is overrun by damn Pigeons!'

This was the town marshal's frustrated retort to Doc when they returned home from the train station. The sight of Marshal Hope striding down the middle of the street, pivoting from side to side with poised shotgun, caused them obvious concern. Doc pulled over his Packard and rolled down the window.

"Good Morning, Dennis, what cha hunting?"

Pigeons were a problem which plagued small towns across America, the dilemma of removing them varied from each community. The solution for this town, at least from their chief, (only) enforcer of the law, was to shoot them on sight.

"Isn't that a bit dangerous? I'm not in the mood for removing buckshot from any neighbor today!"

"Don't worry Doctor, I ordered everyone to stay inside."

"Well, that comforts me!" Doc turned to Morty and rolled his eyes. His sarcastic reply was exemplified by the horrified look on her face. "Let me park my car Dennis and let's chat!"

Doc pulled his car into his back garage and they all three exited.

BANG!' The distinctive sound of a shotgun blast echoed between the Wiseheart grand Victorian style home and the grove of mature maple trees aligning the boundary of their yard. Morty instinctively ran toward the house, while Doc and Pius urgently walked toward the street. The row of trees blocked Doc's vision of the zealously committed town Marshal, and it also blocked the Marshal's vision of them. BOOM!' Just as they arrived at the last tree before the sidewalk, a second blast rang out. This explosive blast brought an aftermath of feathers and leaves showering down upon them.

Doc's initial reaction was to retreat to the safety of his house and join his wife. However, Pius had different thoughts.

So, as Doc spun around to take his first step toward refuge, Pius remained steadfast and shot out like a guided missile toward the street.

"Pius!" Doc's command was futile! By the time Doc had reacted, his dog was at its intended target! Doc immediately ran after Pius!

Another shotgun blast rang out, followed by a barrage of yelling and cursing. When Doc arrived at the sidewalk, he found Marshal Dennis Hope facedown and sprawled out between the walk and the street. His shotgun lay a few feet in front of him on the grass. Standing merciless on the town marshal's back was Pius. At that moment, a flock of pigeons flew a few feet over Hope as if to mock him. A couple of disgruntled fowl had the audacity to drop some excrement on him as they departed over the rooftops and trees.

Doc walked over to the cussing and flailing Marshal.

"Pius! Get off his back!"

With Doc's command, Marshal Hope realized who was responsible for his precarious predicament and adjusted his vengeance accordingly.

"Get your damn mut off me!" He screamed.

Pius turned his head around and inquisitively looked at Doc, as if to confirm his master's intent. Doc extended his arm and pointed.

"Off!"

Pius turned back around, lowered his mouth inches from the back of the Marshal's head and gave him a nasty parting growl. Begrudgingly he jumped off but walked over to the shotgun leaned over and grabbed the red barrel between his K-9 teeth. Without any other delay, he exited the scene with weapon in tow.

"Damn you and your dog!"

Marshal Hope was furious! Still cussing and yelling, he raised himself up just enough to pull his knees up under his frame making it easier to lift his body the rest of the way to his feet. Once erect, he dusted himself off, reached down grabbed his hat and walked over to within inches of Doc. The marshal's face was beet red. He stammered a bit as he delivered his message to Doc.

"You are responsible for your dog and your dog just assaulted a duly appointed officer of the law. I should arrest you for his crime, but instead, I will be back to collect your mut and take him to Doc Power to be put to sleep. You know, the hell with that, I'll just take him out south of town and shoot him myself! Speaking of shooting, where's my damn shotgun?"

"Calm down Dennis! Pius didn't assault you, he merely thought that that he was protecting Morty and I."

"Why don't you come inside, and I'll look you over? My goodness, your blood has rushed to your face. I'll give you something to calm you down before you have a stroke."

"Forget about that, Doctor Wiseheart! I am not coming inside. I'm going back to get my van and another shotgun! Then I'm coming back to impound your dog and then continue shooting more pigeons! If you stand in my way, I'll have to arrest you. If your Dog attacks me again, I'll shoot him dead!"

"Well, I guess you gotta do what cha gotta do! I can't make you come inside either, Dennis. However, I must ask you, did you honestly think the best option to eradicate the Pigeon population was to walk from house to house shooting into the trees? Did you not expect that would cause any issues? Did the thought of being surrounded by houses, people and pets ever cross your mind? Let me ask you Marshal, isn't your first duty and responsibility to protect the citizens of North Salem? Shouldn't you be keeping us safe and out of harm's way?

What if there would have been a young boy up in one of those, that you were shooting into? You know how boys love to climb trees?"

"Why Marshal, I think you may have been neglecting

your duties, maybe even breaking the law! You know I sit on the Town Board. How do you think the rest of the board members would react to your randomly shooting at trees and such?"

Marshal Hope's temper had escalated to a point far beyond common sense. He stammered, kicked the ground, walked away a few yards, turned, and then walked back to within inches of Doc again. This time he was more animated than before, using hand gestures and pointing.

"Let me tell you something Doctor!" The marshal extended his finger on his right hand and began thumping Doc on his chest while he presented his indignant retort.

"You're damn right! The safety of this community is my responsibility and that is why I have taken it upon myself to rid this town of these dirty, filthy, disease infested flying rats! Did you Doctor Wiseheart, not realize that these birds shit everywhere, and their shit is full of disease? What kind of doctor are you? My only options as I see it are to either shoot or poison them. If you have any better idea on how to get rid of them,

I would love to hear about it! Maybe you'd like me to put poison around everywhere."

"Oh, one more thing Doc. You had better keep your dog inside and never let him out of your sight. I would hate to hear about him coming up missing!" With that final ill-conceived comment, the Marshal stormed away.

The town marshal was correct. North Salem did have a pigeon problem. Despite the hostile rhetoric between the men, Doc Wiseheart realized this too. The issue wasn't the plague of pigeons, it was how to get rid of them safely. Neither option that Marshal Hope presented was very attractive. Especially open season with a shotgun! Doc knew that he needed to act quickly before the marshal went on his next rampage, so he called a meeting of the town board.

The board consisted of seven men from the community but the invitees to the meetings generally included the Marshal and the town manager. Both were paid employees.

Pius joined Doc, just as he had in all the meetings prior. Wherever Doc goes, Pius is at his side, everywhere that is, except for church. However, this time he debated whether or not to go solo because of the contentious situation with Marshal Hope. He decided that sooner or later their paths would cross, and the sooner they would get that incident behind them, the better.

Doc was hopeful that Marshal Hope would have cooled down and, perhaps apologize for his overreaction and most importantly, his verbal threat to Pius. Well, that was his hope, but that is not how it played out! When Doc and Pius walked into the townhall boardroom, the already seated Marshal became very indignant! He stood up immediately tipping his chair over and screamed at Doc. "Get that damn dog out of here or I'm leaving!" Doc's jaw dropped from the unanticipated greeting. He looked directly at Marshal Hope, but was speechless. Then he quickly scanned the members in attendance. They were stunned by his outburst!

"What's going on?" One member shouted. "Pius doesn't have to leave!" Another member asserted.

"It's okay gentlemen!" Doc spoke sternly to the room

without taking his eyes off of the marshal. He then looked down at Pius who was already looking back at him.

"Pius, please wait for me outside!" Doc pointed to the door and his dog reluctantly lumbered over to the door and allowed an awaiting member to let him out.

"Now, Dennis, can we conduct a civilized meeting like adults, free from yelling and screaming?" Marshal Hope didn't acknowledge Doc's direct question. He said nothing, picked up his chair, sat down and scooted it up to the table.

The acting chairman banged a wooden gavel on the table and the meeting began. All seven members and the town manager were puzzled by the combative drama between Doctor Wiseheart and Marshal Dennis Hope, but the answers as to why would have to wait.

The Chairman turned to Doc and nodded, giving him a signal to address the group.

"Thanks everyone for showing up today. As you all

are aware the population of pigeons in our town is out of control.

You can't walk ten feet down the sidewalk downtown without stepping in bird droppings. The porches of the homes are covered as well, by the roosting birds along the roofline and gutters. As you know pigeons are a leading carrier of pathogens which cause disease. They are a health menace. They are dirty and disgusting, and we are meeting today to discuss ideas of how to rid our community of this problem. The term 'rid' may be unrealistic, but our goal should be nothing short of substantially reducing the population. What are some ideas which we can discuss today that we can implement quickly and safely?"

"Let's shoot the damn things!" Shouted one of the members, followed by the immediate clapping of Marshal Hope.

"Great idea, but our good doctor here thinks that's too dangerous! I think his damn dog is too dangerous!

Let's talk about me shooting him in the head next time I see him running around!"

The chairman's gavel came crashing down. "Mr. Hope, you are out of order! One more outburst like that and you'll be asked to leave!"

Doc said nothing, he just shook his head. The chairman looked down the table toward Doc.

"Please continue Doc."

"I don't think that there is any ordinance in the book that states you can't shoot a firearm/shotgun within the city limits, but I personally think that's not the safest method." The board member who initially suggested this spoke again. "Yah you are probably right. We can't have everyone shooting up the town." Other members chimed in and shared similar thoughts.

"Well we can't stop homeowners from shooting the birds, as we know several are already doing so. It's their property and it's their right. Saying that, we don't necessarily need to promote it either.

I certainly don't think we should have our town

marshal walking from yard to yard shooting into the trees, either. As a representative of this town, that's not our right!" All heads turned and looked in the direction of Dennis Hope to await his response, but there was none. Just a grunt sound under his breath.

"Another option is poison. There also is an inherent risk with using poison. Perhaps we can regulate it better and distribute it on the rooftops of the building's downtown. I still have concern over the homeowners putting out poison, but once again, we can't infringe on their rights. There are some safer things which we might promote to the homeowners. Things that may be purchased from the hardware store. Wire, spikes, spinning wheels that can be attached on the roofline or gutters. These items could cause the birds to seek alternative places to roost. Higher and out of the way! The trick would be to have them populate up to the water tower. I have seen several birds already up there. It's an ideal location. Pigeons love high cliff like settings.

I think the only reason more are not roosting up there

is that it's farther away from their food source of seeds and berries. Maybe with a combination of frightening devices on the homes and the placement of seed/suet bags on the tower, we can encourage them to go there." This idea presented by Doc caused a lot of enthusiasm at the table. Except from, of course, the Marshal.

"While you all are planning your fantasy pigeon roundup, I'll look into getting the poison!"

With that Marshal Hope stood up glaring at Doc, then stormed out of the room. Outside of the town hall, he once again encountered his nemesis stretched out under a tree. The marshal abruptly stopped, walked over in front of Pius, drew his service revolver, and pointed it directly at the lying dog. 'Click'

"Next time mut, you won't hear that sound, there'll be a bullet in the chamber and you'll be dead!" Pius snarled and then barked, sending the marshal on his way.

The board meeting concluded with a clear strategy and request for immediate implementation. Flyers were to be written and distributed with the suggestions of implementing wire barbs or metallic spinners. Also, a paragraph was added asking homeowners with birdfeeders to temporarily cease maintaining the compartments with seed. The town manager was tasked with climbing the water tower with bags of grease and sunflower seeds. The town marshal, Dennis Hope did obtain large volumes of rat poison and did distribute it liberally on the roof tops. He acted solely and without oversight. It was speculated that he laced seed bags similar to those used on the tower with the poison and scattered them on top of each building. It was also speculated that he didn't confine his operation to the roof tops as directed.

Several bags were found dangling from trees.

Within a few days of implementing their assault on the pigeon population, results were realized. Despite very few homes displaying devices to scare away the feathered vermin, their plan was working! Working all too well and to the dismay of many!

The water tower was gray with hundreds of pigeons, so many that their flocking was covering up the boldly painted name North Salem on the tank. Below the tank, the beams of the support frame were white with streams of droppings. Beneath the shadow of the tower, the yard was damp, saturated with pigeon urine and feces. Throughout the town, the streets, walks and yards were littered with the remains of the fallen. Dead pigeons were everywhere! If that wasn't bad enough, the situation got worse. Soon after, dead cats, presumed to have been eating the poisoned birds were also appearing all over town. Sadly, many were house cats, pets, and they returned home to die.

The do-gooders of the town, in an attempt to eliminate a problem, made it worse!

"We need wood boxes to bury the cats and birds!" The town manager sent out letters to the board members pleading for resources to collect and dispose of the poisoned.

Three weeks after the initial pigeon meeting, another was called. For this meeting, the topic was dealing with the aftermath.

Once again, flyers were written and distributed, thanking the town for helping eliminate the pigeon population. More importantly, suggesting that their efforts cease to allow proper cleanup and disposal. The flyer danced around the dead cat issue, saying that they were investigating why some cats in the community were also dying. Even though it was common knowledge that most of the pigeons were poisoned, there was no mention of the poison. Instead, a carefully crafted sentence suggested that the cat carnage was most likely due to contact with the diseased birds.

The Trustees of the Board allocated money as requested to the town manager to quickly collect and dispose of the cats and birds. They suggested that he be as discrete as possible. He was discrete and with the help of Marshal Hope, they ended up burying the wooden boxes under the water tower, which was blocked from sight by the town hall building. Something else was disposed of as well.

Fearing possible retribution from the community over the poisoning of much of the town's feline population, both feral and domesticated, the Marshal decided it was prudent to dispose of the remaining rat poison too. Nearly 200 gallons of toxic liquid in metal canasters were placed on top of the wood boxes and were covered with dirt.

The dimensions of the hole needed to dispose of the boxes plus the 40 five-gallon cans was significant. They ended up using the town's rubber-tired backhoe to do most of the excavation and backfilling.

"Aren't you worried about the cans rusting and the poison draining down into the town water well?" It was a legitimate question the town manager asked Marshal Hope as they stood on top of the bank, peering down into the hole. It was a question which should have been asked long before now. It was a legitimate question that neither man considered before now. The Marshal was slow to respond to his counterpart, as he didn't have a good answer.

"Oh well, what the Hell, not our problem! By the time those cans rust through, you and I will be long dead!" The Marshal realized he wasn't trying to convince the town board, just the town manager, and it sufficed.

All of the cans were buried, but not all of the poison.

Marshal Hope didn't bury all the poison, because he had one remaining animal that he needed to destroy. The night before the disposal project, he filled a glass Ball jar with what he deemed sufficient for his dark task, then sealed the can and returned it to the lot before disposing.

"So, Doctor Cadwallader Wells, I've been meaning to ask you, where did you find Doc Wiseheart's medical bag? I had it locked away in a closet with a few of his personal items that came with the estate. A couple of years ago, I discovered it missing, but I had no idea when the theft occurred. I assumed that a guest pilfered it from the closet, but I thought it strange that that was all they took."

"I didn't find the medical bag, it found me! I woke to it sitting on the end of the bed. Perhaps this is a good time to tell me more about Doctor Wiseheart and his dog." Caddy looked up at Myrna as she was delivering him a mid-morning coffee to his desk.

"Well, you've been here for almost five days and

this is, I think, the third time you've asked me that same exact question.

Each time one of us got sidetracked and you never got the chance to hear my response." She laughed.

"You realize that I am not a historian or authority of all things North Salem. I'm just like, so many others who lived here all of their lives, I can only pass along things I've heard." Caddy took a sip of his coffee, smiled, and nodded. "I accept your disclaimer, Ms. Wilson! Humor me with your insightful lore!"

"Well, here's a quick rundown. Doc Wiseheart practiced here for over 50 years. He was loved and cherished by everyone. He delivered most of the babies in town including myself. He treated everyone for everything, from stitches and broken bones to pneumonia!

"Outside of our community Doc was known for his treatment of rheumatoid arthritis. People would come from hundreds of miles to receive injections to relieve their symptoms. I still remember the long lines outside of this building nearly every day.

"I think he passed in 1967 and was preceded in death by his wife Morty by a few years. Her death devastated him! Actually, it was the combination of her and his beloved dog Pius, both dying within a couple of days of the other. He quit practicing shortly after she died, claiming if he couldn't save his own wife, he wasn't worthy of having the title of physician!" Myrna hesitated giving time for Caddy to respond.

"He sounds like an amazing man! I'm envious, I would have loved to practice medicine in his era! The days of small-town doctors are long gone. Such a different time. Medicine has progressed tremendously, but sadly doctor-patient relationships have declined. As a member of that community I can testify, we are in such a hurry and don't take time to develop personal bonds!" Caddy continued.

"You know what I really want to know."

"You want to know about Pius, don't you? You are one of the few who have ever seen his spirit. More than that, you actually have a relationship, a bond!

He selected you. Maybe he's excited to have a doctor back in his house. Perhaps you remind him of his master, Doctor Oscar Wiseheart. Perhaps he wants you to take care of something. Maybe some unfinished business."

"Pius was a rare Fox Red Labrador. A red dog!"

"Red dog! Isn't the tavern downtown called, The Red Dog? There must be a connection, right?" Caddy was all ears! He sat his coffee down and leaned up in his seat.

"Yes, the establishment was named after the infamous Pius. The name Red Dog sounds a whole lot more inviting than The Pius! Don't you think?" She laughed.

"Did you say that Pius died approximately the same time as Doc's wife?"

"Yes, Morty died of cancer and Pius was poisoned!"

"Intentionally poisoned?" Caddy responded.

"I don't know all of the details, but yes, that's the lore. Maybe that's why he's not at rest. Whoever it was must have really hated the dog, or Doc, or both."

"Interesting! So, I'm guessing that they never caught the thug?"

Myrna shrugged her shoulders and shook her head.

"As a kid, I do remember hearing about the town controlling the pigeon population with poison. Even a few cats died after eating the dead pigeons. Maybe Pius got into some of the poison."

'*Buzz*'! Caddy was alerted to an email. He glanced down at the phone sitting on the table.

"It's the lab! Not the dog, but the hospital laboratory in Chicago!" He snickered, then continued to read and scroll.

"What's it say?" Myrna's voice cracked with anticipation.

"Bloodwork results of Connie and Harley Goode!

Inconclusive. Possible histoplasmosis but also traces of anticoagulants."

"Antico what?" A confused look came upon Myrna.

"Rodenticide." Caddy stammered a bit as he was concentrating on reading the email and responding to Myrna.

"They had traces of rat poison in their blood!"

"You don't think it could be the rat poison used in the 1960's, do you? That couldn't be possible. Could it?" Myrna was shocked, listening to Caddy just moments after recalling her childhood memories of the town's use of poison. "A coincidence or a premonition", the thought flashed through her mind.

"I'm sure it's just a coincidence, Myrna! It's been at least sixty years, right? As I said, there were also traces of antigens associated with histoplasmosis. The amount of rodenticide and histo-antigens are low enough as to not cause death with most healthy people, but they will make you sick."

"I need to get the rest of the lab results back from the others to confirm a pattern or cause, and then we can look for the source or sources. That is, the source of the poison as well as the cause of the histoplasmosis."

Myrna looked at her watch and stood up.

"Look at the time! I need to get back to the house and start fixing us something to eat."

"Not tonight!" Caddy responded.

"What do you say about letting me treat you to a steak at the Red Dog tavern?"

A great big smile immediately formed on Myrna's face.

"You smell the filets grilling over the applewood, don't you?" She teased.

In the short period of time since Caddy's arrival to North Salem, he had gained a plethora of new friends while acting as the new town doctor. As soon as they walked through the door of the local watering hole and eatery, Caddy was inundated with greetings and well wishes. They were escorted to a small booth adjacent to the long bar. Before they were introduced to their waitress the bartender arrived with a bottle of cabernet and two glasses.

"To the Queen of North Salem, Myrna Wilson, I present my finest bottle of California red. I would be honored to meet your guest!"

"But, of course!" She looked at Caddy. "Doctor Cadwallader Wells, may I introduce you to the proprietor of this wonderful establishment, Donald Booker."

"I'm honored! Well we finally meet! I think that I'm the only person in town that you haven't taken blood from."

He let out a barrel laugh that turned every head his way. "You even treated my ill wife and took blood from her and my son."

"He also treated several of these gents filling the stools behind you. Or at least someone in their family." Myrna opined and he nodded his head in agreement.

Caddy stood up and extended his hand.

"The honor is mine and please call me Caddy!"

He set the bottle and glasses on the table.

"Call me Booker!" With exuberant fury he grabbed Caddy's hand, gripped hard and shook.

"Sit! Tonight, you dine as my guest. Tomorrow, I'll drop by to see you and we'll talk about my wife and son's blood results. I may even let you take my blood, too!"

Caddy and Myrna graciously obliged, setting in motion the impromptu gala of food and beverage.

Soon, every barstool and table was taken and the aisleway between was occupied to the limit, leaving little space to maneuver. The seats were full, but not stagnant.

Tonight's clientele, with their alternating posteriors took turns visiting Caddy and Myrna's table. Most brought Caddy good tidings, accompanied with an adult beverage. Some brought advice and counsel compliments of alcohol inducement, but none so much as his new friend and substitute mother, Myrna.

"So why is this handsome, successful doctor not married? That is the question on every woman's mind here, you know. You are not gay, are you?"

"Would you like me any less if I were?" Caddy leaned over the table as if he were about to break a secret. The occupants at the table suddenly went silent.

"No! Of course not!" She blurted out. The others responded awkwardly in the same fashion.

"Well, that's good to know! Oh, by the way, I'm not!

Rest assured that if I were, there's not any males here in this community that I would be attracted to!" Caddy waved his arm around the room displaying the men to make his case.

"Amen to that!" Myrna was quick to opine. The two male guests at the table weren't so quick to respond, but when they grasped Caddy's sarcastic comeback, they burst out in laughter. "We got ugly women too! *Except for you of course Mrs. Wilson.*" The table erupted again.

Booker made several trips to the table as well. Usually after escorting an overserved individual to the door. There were no cabs in North Salem, so Caddy's inquiry as to how they got home went unanswered.

"So, Booker, tell me a story or two about the Red Dog. Not your building, but the dog that you presumably named it after."

Myrna spoke up. "I think what Caddy wants to know is, have you ever saw the dog Pius?"

"If I say yes will you have me committed?" Booker laughed, and Myrna replied for Caddy.

"Don't worry, Book! He has seen him just like you and me. He's now struggling with that fact!

"In that case, what she said! He usually follows me when I walk home after closing."

Caddy stared inquisitively at his new friend but didn't reply.

Booker reached into his pocket and pulled out his phone.

"Sorry folks, I got to run home. The wife is

summonsing me." He jumped up and yelled some instructions to his assistant behind the bar and darted out.

The evening could have continued forever, but the Doctor and his date wisely decided that their night was over. Before Booker left, he instructed his bar to comp their bill. Final handshakes and hugs were delivered, and Caddy and Myrna set out on their short walk back to the bed and breakfast.

"I wonder if Pius followed Booker home tonight?" Caddy's question broke the silence of their walk.

"He had plenty of time to see him home and return for us. I caught you sneaking a peek a few steps back." Myrna reached over and playfully patted him on the shoulder.

"Yah, not so fortunate! I guess he knows you're safe with me."

"I suppose!"

The night was dark, but the sidewalks were illuminated by streetlamps to safely guide them back. When they arrived at the, Caddy gestured

Myrna to walk ahead of him up the walk to her door. As a gentleman he reached around, pulled open the screen while she unlocked the door, and she walked through. Once she crossed the threshold the screen door suddenly broke free from his hand and slammed shut. Myrna was startled and quickly turned around. The confused Doctor reached out and grabbed the handle again but this time to door wouldn't budge.

Just then Caddy felt a familiar feeling from behind. It was the feeling of paws jumping on his back nudging him forward.

"It's Pius!" Myrna shouted.

Caddy spun around to find the dark shadow of the dog staring at him.

"What's wrong boy?" Instinctively Caddy spoke to the image, triggering it to spin around and run off the porch. Without hesitation Caddy followed. Simultaneously, the screen door released its lock on Myrna, so she joined the pursuit.

'Pius', she yelled. "Where are you taking us?"

The image was faint and several paces ahead of them, but it never let them lose sight. Its gait was urgent and so was Caddy and Myrna's to keep up. Their destination was in sight. One house stood out in the late hours of the pitch-black night, as it was illuminated by every light being on.

"It's the Booker house!" She had barely enough breath left to announce this, but Myrna managed to alert Caddy. It must have been where Pius intended them to be. Suddenly, he was no longer visible. Caddy reached out his arm and grabbed Myrna's shoulder, stopping her.

He pointed ahead to another shadowy image walking down the sidewalk of the illuminated home. It appeared to be a man and was presumed to be Booker. In one hand he was carrying a shovel, and it the other a satchel. Caddy sensed Myrna's desire to speak, so he quickly intervened by putting his index figure over his mouth showing her his intension to be unnoticed. The streetlamp revealed that it was Booker, but he did not see them standing in the shadows. The situation with Pius leading them here to witness this was very bizarre.

Caddy's instinct was compelling him just to observe.

They hung back a block or so and followed Booker back downtown. His trek went past his Red Dog establishment, then strangely took a beehive diagonally across the deserted street toward the Water Tower.

Not once in his journey did he look back or even from side to side to see if he were being followed. His demeanor was not of a man who was committing a crime, which gave Caddy comfort.

"It looks like he's going to burry a pet" Myrna whispered.

"How do you know that?"

"Well, he has a shovel and he's headed for the graveyard." Caddy stopped, turned, and looked directly into Myrna's eyes with open mouth.

"You mean to tell me that there's a pet cemetery

underneath the water tower? Is that where Pius is buried too?"

"Oh no, Pius is buried out at Wilson's Woods!"

"Okay, it's getting way too late. I'm tired and I can't process any more information. Apparently, Mr. Booker is not committing a crime, so we don't need to call the sheriff.

I suggest we conclude this adventure and head back. Sleep is long overdue! Tomorrow, you can tell me about the pet graves and Wilsons Woods.

Just like every morning prior, hot coffee was waiting for Caddy when he appeared from his room. This morning, the scent of freshly brewed coffee was accompanied by the aroma of crescent rolls.

"Good morning, Mrs. Wilson!" Caddy walked directly over to the coffee pot, grabbed the container and poured the steaming brew into the awaiting cup.

"Wilsons Woods was a 5-star campground just west of town. My father carved it out of a forest many years ago. People would travel and camp there from all parts of America and other countries. When my parents' health deteriorated thirty years ago, they closed the gate."

Caddy walked over to the table, pulled out his chair and sat down.

"You're picking up where we left off last night and I didn't even have to ask. All before my first sip of Folgers!"

He smiled and raised his cup at Myrna. "I assumed that Wilsons Woods was your family's property. Very nice! You must have many a fond memory! I'm glad that you led off our discussion!"

"You commented several days ago that Pius was poisoned. Why did they choose to bury him at your family's campground?" Caddy blew into his cup in an attempt to cool its contents and waited for her to respond.

"The town loved Pius, and most were devastated by his sudden passing. Doc and Morty would take Pius out from town often and let him run in our woods. He loved Wilson's Woods! Doc asked my mother and father if he could make a spot somewhere in the woods his final resting place. Of course, they said yes! Some say he spends his days frolicking in the ravines chasing rabbits. Actually, it's not 'some', it's me! I was very young when Pius died. However, I do remember my parents taking me to Doctor Wiseheart and how Pius would sit beside me. I remember one time how terrified I was to get a shot of some sort and Pius crawled up in my lap to comfort me."

"That wasn't the last time Pius consoled me. I used to see Pius often when I walked. That was later in my childhood." Myrna stopped to recall a memory and her eyes filled.

"I would always go into the woods to sort out my thoughts. I think I was fourteen, I had a terrible crush on this boy in school, so I wrote him a note. Bad decision! Not only did he reject me, he shared my private thoughts with his friends. They all laughed and made fun of me. I was devastated! I couldn't wait to get home. I ran from the bus and went directly into the woods. I remember sitting on a log and crying my eyes out. That is, until I felt his warm breath. I looked up, startled, but that emotion along with my grief, instantly disappeared. There was Pius, sitting right in front of me. I remember his big brown eyes staring into mine, as if he understood all of my emotions." Myrna took in a deep breath and sighed. "Other than my late husband, I don't think that I have told anyone that story before!"

"Oh, by-the-way, town folk have only been burying their family pets under the water tower for the last couple of decades."

"That was a beautiful story! Thank you for sharing!"

Caddy took another sip of his coffee, reached into his pocket and pulled out his phone. For a few minutes he stared, studied and scrolled. Then he pushed his chair away from the table and stood up.

"Myrna, would you show me the Pet cemetery? I've got a feeling that our red dog wants me to see it!"

"Was that him that emailed you?" She smiled and he laughed.

"No, just more reports from the lab. It seems just about everyone including the Booker women have different degrees of rodenticide in their blood. It looks like some even have antigens similar to that associated with histoplasmosis."

"Oh, my Lord! Are they going to die?" Myrna's voice trembled with terror.

"The toxins are certainly capable of killing, however, it looks like most of the amounts that I see are low enough not to be lethal. Just enough to make you very sick!"

"You did tell me a while back that there has been an increase in deaths to the elderly. The elderly that I checked that are positive do seem to be the sickest. So, perhaps it's taking a toll on those who are the weakest!"

"Let's go for that walk." She nodded.

The normal time for a four-block hike to the tower should have taken a few minutes, however it was morning and the streets were a bustle. Not just with grain trucks heading to the mill, but with local pedestrians walking to the bank, post office and mini mart. Everyone they crossed paths with insisted on chatting or having a quick sidewalk exam from the doctor.

Finally, they reached their destination. 'The true stature and girth of the silver structure is not realized until you are standing beneath it and looking up.' This was the first thought that rushed into Caddy's mind as he stood in the grass alongside Myrna.

The massive steel tank was supported by four rectangular steel girder posts and set perched nearly one hundred fifty vertical feet into the sky. Each three by three post was sixty foot apart from the other, creating a surface of grass thirty-six hundred square. There was a small area of churned up dirt, just outside of the perimeter. Caddy pointed to it.

"That looks like a small grave!"

"Yes, I'm afraid that the inside area has filled up and is now overflowing beyond the shade of the tower."

"So how did this all come about, burying pets under the tower?" Caddy asked.

"Well, I think it caught on after our town marshal buried a bunch of dead cats and pigeons."

"Yah, the dumb bastard poisoned them!"

A third voice interjected from behind. Both Caddy and Myrna simultaneously spun around to find Booker standing a few feet away.

"Booker!" Myrna screamed. "You scared the Hell out of us!"

"I see you're giving our guest a tour of the pet graveyard. I'm sure that he's thrilled!" Booker stood there with a smirk on his face and holding a bouquet of daisies.

"Well, I had to visit this place last night. Our cat finally passed away. She gave it a good fight and spent all of her nine lives. The wife and daughter are devastated. My daughter picked these flowers and wanted me to place them on her grave. My wife thought it was best she not come with me this soon. Maybe when my wife feels better, we can all three come and visit."

"Booker, did you say that the town marshal poisoned the cats? Yes, I think it was an accident, but still..."

It was like an epiphany! Caddy looked up at the tower and then back at the ground.

"Is the well that fills the tower below here?"

"Well, yes Sherlock! What do you think that pipe is running out of the ground and up to the tank?" Didn't graduate at the top of your class, did you?"

Caddy ignored Booker's sarcastic razzing.

"When was the last time that the State Board of Health or the IDEM tested the town's water?"

"Hell, I don't know, never!" Booker shrugged.

"Well, I'm calling them now! You two are going to help me collect water samples from about a dozen homes. Myrna, the agencies will collect their own samples, but I want to send them off to my laboratory too."

"Booker, later we are going to do some excavating! Does the town have a backhoe?"

"It's a pile of rust! Don't worry, I'll have you one that works, with an operator, this afternoon!"

"I'm going to need the town's permission, as well as witnesses. Round up board members and the new marshal!"

"Not a problem! I'm chairman of the Town Board!"

"Great!"

"And, you don't remember if the water has ever been checked!" Caddy shook his head and Booker hung his in shame.

"Myrna, you're going to need plastic sealed containers or cups. Write down the address and homeowner's name and have them sign it. I only need three or four ounces. Try to get the samples on different streets!" She nodded.

As soon as Caddy instructed his newly formed team of their orders, they were off. The need for urgency was never mentioned, as it was very apparent and obvious!

Caddy had his own assignment and perhaps it was the hardest. Trying to get in touch of the right person at a government agency who actually cares and would respond immediately wasn't easy!

After multiple calls and emails including a joint call with Booker and the town marshal the Indiana Department of Environmental Management agreed to send out an emergency response crew.

News traveled quick. A crowd of thirty or so gathered under the tower, all to watch one man slowly excavate a grave sized hole. On the banks paralleling the pit, stood two men in white hazard suits, the town marshal, Booker and Caddy. The pit got deeper, and the pile of dirt got higher. Every scoop, the two white suites took samples.

Finally, a metallic scraping noise caught the attention of the group. Immediately the gallery became animated with hand gestures and pointing causing the backhoe to stop. One of the men jumped down into the hole with a shovel. Booker yelled. "It's a can! Several cans!"

After sixty years, Marsal Dennis Hope's rusty cache of poison was unearthed!

Immediately, the area was taped off and the onlookers were escorted away. Samples of the toxic liquid were taken, and emergency cleanup crews were called in.

It was confirmed that the liquid still left in the rusted cans was rodenticide, rat poison.

Hundreds of gallons of the toxic liquid seeped through the compromised metal cans down into the aquifer. The water well would ultimately pull the water into the tower for potable distribution through the town. The surrounding soil samples confirmed this activity had been going on for months, potentially a year or two.

It took three days for hazmat crews to remove what was left of the rusted cans, rotted wood and, sadly, the bones and remains of hundreds of pets.

Myrna's water samples sent to Caddy's laboratory, coinciding with the state agency's findings, which confirmed contaminated water.

For an unidentified amount of time, the town had been bathing and drinking rat poison!

Caddy's work was finished! He stayed at the Bed-and -Breakfast for a couple of more days to check on his recent patients and to attend a Ratoberfest party downtown on the street. The off-humor event was to celebrate life, those who had passed and those who survived. The guest of honor, of course was Doctor Wells, who they gave a key to the city plaque, carved by a local furniture builder and blessed by the four churches.

It was time for Caddy to return to Evanston. Fate may have brought him to this small town and a mysterious K-9 Spirit coaxed him to stay, but Evanston was his home and Evanston was where he practiced medicine. Nevertheless, Caddy acquired a second home and a new group of friends! Even an adopted family!

One in particular, Caddy gave a long embrace to his second mother, or what Myrna preferred he say, his older sister.

Caddy jumped in his car and headed out of town the way he arrived. It was a beautiful morning and he was looking forward to an easy drive home. His trip home had just started when he noticed the big tree that he was so rudely introduced to on his arrival. There was one more thing that he didn't notice on his earlier trip but recognized just the same. There it was! Despite the foliage, a large wood sign with dynamic yellow letters stood out. *WILSONS WOODS!*

"I've gotta stop!" Caddy slowed up and did a U-turn, then pulled off the shoulder and stopped. "I've got time to do a quick walk around before I head back." He was justifying his actions to himself, all while recalling Myrna's childhood story. He felt he needed to see the landscape for himself.

Caddy climbed over the chain across the drive and hiked a short distance to the top of the hill.

There were many trees, weeds and briars that made it difficult to maneuver. He did come across the remains of some wood structures, which were dilapidated with the roofs collapsed. One he surmised to once be the living quarters of Myrna's parents.

Caddy came to a natural opening in the trees. Before him was a deep ravine and at the bottom was a stream.

"Breathtaking beauty!" He thought. There was a fallen log off to his side. He decided he'd sit for five minutes and absorb this scenic image before returning to his car to head home. So, he sat! Five minutes became fifteen minutes, and it would have been longer, but something happened.

Caddy felt a sudden wet sensation on the back

of his neck, prompting him to jump to his feet and spin around.

"Pius!" He shouted with joy. Standing wagging his tail was the dog. "I thought that I wouldn't get the chance to say goodbye!"

Pius lowered his head and picked something off the ground and approached Caddy as if he wanted to give it to him. Caddy extended his arms in an attempt to pat his head, but the vision was gone. He disappeared! However, what was in his mouth didn't. It fell from his mouth to the ground at Caddy's feet.

Despite Caddy witnessing Pius's disappearing act before, it was something he could not get accustomed to. He stood frozen in his tracks for several seconds, trying to absorb what had happened, trying to justify whether it was real or a figment of his mind. Caddy looked down at his feet and the item that was in Pius's mouth was laying there for him to pick up. He leaned over and gently retrieved it, bringing it close to his face to inspect. Tears rolled down the doctor's cheeks. The item which Pius presented to Caddy was a leather dog collar and inscribed on a gold plate was, *Pius, loving dog of Doctor Oscar Wiseheart, North Salem, Indiana.*

THE END

North Salem is my hometown. I have lots of fond memories and feel blessed to have had a childhood nurtured by this loving and supportive community.

I had no personal encounters with Doc Wiseheart, as I was very young when he passed. However, I certainly have witnessed his impact.

Writing this story was a labor of love for me!

Even though North Salem is a real town in Central Indiana and Doctor Wiseheart was genuine, the storyline I wrote is totally fiction! I took the liberty of collecting names from my past and giving them to my created characters. I did mix in a few real events to tease my hometown fans.

Enjoy!

Scott Baker Sweeney

Special thanks to Jan Whiteman,
Joan Hamilton Ott, and
Michele Wiles for contributing
valuable information.

OSCAR H. WISEHEART, M.D. - Among those men of sterling attributes of character who have impressed their personality upon the community of their residence and have borne their full share in the upbuilding and development of Hendricks County, mention must not be omitted of Dr. Oscar H. Wiseheart, of North Salem, Indiana.

Doc Wiseheart maintained his home and exerted a strong influence for good on the entire community. He was a man of upright principles and desirous to see the advancement of the community along moral, educational and material lines. Professionally, he is a man of recognized ability, who has in his chosen sphere of effort met with a large degree of success, winning the commendation and the confidence of all who have knowledge of the great value of the competent physician to any community.

Oscar Wiseheart was a man of character and strong Christian faith! He was thoughtful and forthright, traits that connected him to the community. Doc, as he was lovingly known as, was a man who inspired confidence which is as necessary to the patient as are the medicines which are given by the physician. His personality was pleasing and the deep sympathy which he felt for his patients was apparent.

He exemplified a 'Small town Doctor!